Natalsa of the Brim
Chad McClendon

NATALSA OF THE BRIM

Cover art and design by Jerry8448 (jerry8448.deviantart.com) as
well as Lisa Swenne (wolfke74.deviantart.com/).

+ DEDICATION +

This book is dedicated to my mother, Teresa McClendon, who taught me the magic of reading and writing.

It is also dedicated to my father, Michael McClendon, whose paycheck afforded my love of reading for so long.

+ Prologue +

IT WAS THE FIRST time my magic failed me, or perhaps I failed my magic. It was hard to believe in anything when all around me the fools were burning our portion of the town, and smoke rolled through the alleyways. I pulled my cowl closer to cover my face, not daring to be discovered with the current state of things, but my knife was ready in case I had to do the unthinkable.

I looked over my shoulder, and in the dancing flames light I saw a group of youths tossing a witch's Familiar around, and I gasped as I saw one of them fling the cat as far into the air as they could. I turned my eyes before it reached the damning ground, I could not bear to hear its death.

To the shadows I clung, taking brief refuge in the darkness, as all around me the world I loved was on the border of collapse. I shuddered, and urged myself to move. I peeked around a corner, and waited for a mob to pass, they were drunk, whiskey filled the air along with derogatory slurs against my kind. I exited the alley and bumped right into another person, we both fell backwards. I was the first to recover, but the other was right behind me.

He rose to his feet, and noticed my face, and his eyes gleamed in recognition. "Natalsa of the Brim, and here I was thinking you'd be dead already." He said, as he reached into his jacket and pulled out a cord of rope and a bag of white powder. "I bind thee, witch, by the powers of righteousness. Stand and speak not, or I will end you."

He moved towards me, and I could not be taken. I drew my dagger and lashed at his wrists, spurts of life sprayed from his arms and he cried out in anger. It was enough to slow him down, and enough to get me out alive and not be a murderer, for such would fan their pyres against me. I look around my city, and from behind me I heard the cries of others being hunted, being tied, and being burned. Oh yes, on a night like tonight, the magic had failed, and I wondered if it had ever been ours to begin with.

✠ BOOK ONE ✠

+ CHAPTER ONE +

NATALSA DRAGGED THE UNCONSCIOUS

stranger to a small rock wall and leaned him carefully against its damp surface. She looked up and down the street, and turned her head this way and that. A mousy scavenger rooted through garbage, but she heard nothing else. The moon hid behind the buildings, and the occasional light that peeked through window panes could not cut through the darkness completely. She trusted that he would be safe enough here, and with a knowledge that he deserved to be left in a worse state, she sighed and covered him with her cloak to keep him from catching his death. After all, to be cloaked would draw attention, and she needed to be as slim as her current chances of survival.

She rubbed her arms rapidly as her skin began to break out in goose bumps and her knees popped in defiance as she hid under a stone wall; her eyes peeked up out from behind it, and saw nothing but moonlight. She saw her shadow creep in front of her as she moved. Her pale scars around both of her wrists were lit up most under direct light, and she saw the mark the demon had left on her. The demon which had caused these problems, Kaltegys. She hoped he was suffering. Cries tore at her ears, and caused her to swivel around. She was still alone, but someone wasn't, and she held her chest in a gesture of solidarity. "Be at peace, sister." She offered the skies a prayer as she heard the screams continue. Her portion of the town was falling to Estil's purge. She had to hurry if she had any chance of getting back to her home and saving anything dear to her. Delia, her familiar, became a primary concern. Her little black kitten was surely peeking from the windows even now. But the antique tea cup and her books were sentimentally important.

She was able to dodge passers-by due to being intimately familiar with the town; she had been raised on these dirt streets, and had hidden in the cornfields since she was just learning knot magic. She held her breath and listened intently, sure that her breath might give her location away. She heard the shouts of mobs directing the drunkards, ordering their movements away from the Witch's Quarters. They reveled in the streets, happy for any reason to cause a ruckus it seemed. "And by the sunlight your deeds will stink worse than the sticky vomit on your frocks." She cursed, and crept past them.

She was nearly to her humble little house when she heard a broken whimper from behind an elder tree. She stopped in her tracks and peered all around her, looking for any indication of a trap. "I really should be running." She scolded herself, and turned reluctantly towards the sound.

"Hello? Declare yourself." She drew her knife, and the hairs on the back of her neck rose as her fingertips tingled. She heard leaves crunching under the feet of another, and braced herself for whatever brute might appear.

She recognized the black-haired girl who peeked out at her from behind the tree. She let herself relax and lowered her knife. "My father is missing, and they've burned my home."

Natalsa inhaled sharply and felt the air cool the words of warding that had been resting on her tongue. "You are Estil's daughter. Yet they have burned your homes?"

"They came with fire in their hands and they were cloaked in nightshroud." The girl gazed at Natalsa, and slowly the trust on her face melted to suspicion. "But, aren't you one of them? Aren't you a witch?"

Natalsa frowned and felt her heart pulse with sadness. "Child, I would do you no harm. You've done no wrong."

"But you are one of them, I recognize you. Father says the witches have had consort with the demons. And that you seek to bring Halflings back into the world."

Natalsa's wrists burned mildly. "The only contact I have with demons is when I send them back to their realm. I promise you." She held out her hands towards the girl.

"Can you help me find father?" She asked, and Natalsa wondered if she knew how silly a request it was.

"I cannot do that, for your father would have me killed, I am sure." She watched the girl carefully. The beginning of sympathy was beginning to grow within her. *Is this a time to have sympathy?* She questioned herself.

She frowned and Natalsa struggled to remember her age. *Ten? Twelve? Older still?* And any of the mob would likely recognize her, and get her to her father. But then again, mobs simply wanted blood most times; they didn't care from whence it came. Natalsa sighed and looked at the girl.

The girl was Emmaline, or so Natalsa thought. She decided to trust her instincts. "Emmaline, come with me, I haven't long, but I will make sure you are safe and sound before I carry on my business."

She heard a shot in the distance, and she clenched her knife until it bit into her palm.

"But remember this, be swift. It would not be good to be seen with me." Emmaline took her hand, it was tiny in Natalsa's and it was trembling.

The two walked in silence from that moment forward, and Natalsa surveyed the area around Estil's house. Long before the manor could be seen, the smoke filled the wind with its stench. Natalsa climbed nimbly up a tree to get a better view, and was not surprised with what she saw. Windows were illuminated by dancing flames, and blackened smoky clouds rose to the heavens.

Natalsa hopped down. "Come, I know somewhere where you could be safe."

Emmaline followed close behind, and several times Natalsa almost tripped over her dress. She heard her dress rip soon thereafter, and she nearly toppled forward.

Natalsa navigated her way through town undetected until she reached the town hall. A vacant noose swung menacingly from the branches of a tall elder tree. Natalsa's stomach turned, and she looked at Emmaline. "You will be safe within these walls, run in, and lock the doors behind you."

Natalsa looked at the girl, and could sense her fear. Suddenly overcome with an urge so strong it nearly knocked her down, she handed Emmaline her knife. She knew the girl wouldn't understand the significance of this gesture, she wouldn't understand that Natalsa had just surrendered her last option to the child. Suicide was better than torture, or the licking flames. But she knew that the girl must take this, even though it was her safety, she couldn't ignore this feeling.

"Take this, and if anyone tries to hurt you, hurt them first."

Emmaline took the knife and looked at it. "Are you leaving me too? Daddy said I would be safe at home, but look what happened there. I'm afraid."

Natalsa's sympathies finally won out, and she frowned. "This knife will keep you safe. It has never failed me in my most dire situations. The Will of the Ancients will protect you child, you are innocence itself." Natalsa kissed the girl on her forehead. "Go now. My protection goes with you, for what its worth on this dreadful night."

"Natalsa, is what my father said true? Are the witches bad?"

Natalsa shook her head without a doubt. "We have protected our villages for over two hundred years. Never once have we sought murder at twilight."

"What does that make my father?"

Natalsa frowned. "Your father loves *you*. There is no doubt of this. Go now."

Emmaline looked back at Natalsa only once, and bounded up the stairs two at a time. After the door shut, Natalsa turned and made haste to reach her own home. She worried that she had dawdled too long, and she worried for her cat.

She raced through the side streets, carrying a growing sense of foreboding. She doubted the mobs had yet reached her house, the witch's quarter was still somewhat large, and the pronouncement had only come at dusk. And she knew a good rabble needed time to get going properly.

She wasn't sure why she was trying to fool herself.

Her small but comfortable home came into view, and the flames were still on torches, and not her woodwork. But a crowd was gathered, and in the center of the crowd was the man she had spared. He leaned against Estil, and he was speaking rapidly.

"Then, I barely escaped Natalsa. I luckily held my protective reagents and kept her at bay. But still, look at my wounds, see her destruction. Her previous acts of heroism aside, she is now an enemy. Just as Estil said she was." He looked over to a tall man in a black uniform. In his hand he held Delia. She meowed and hissed, and scratched at Estil.

"I will speak on her personal account, and declare that if your testimony is true Leon, then she is our enemy and worthy of execution."

The mob expressed its pleasure at this, and laid flames to Natalsa's home. Natalsa watched in silent terror as her home and all her memories went up in smoke. She began to call to mind the words of a spell, but then stopped her whispering. She could no more succeed in casting that spell tonight than she could fly of independent means. Her home held heirlooms, components, her grandmother's library, and so many memories Her lip trembled, and she wished that she could give up on caring about what was happening.

Her one concern was for her cat, and her heart thudded in her chest. Leon, apparently, the name of the man she had assaulted - though she could not recall ever seeing him in town before, was smiling.

"Shall we toss the beast inside as well? Estil?" He pointed at the cat who hissed all the more.

"I see little reason why not, I do not know what hold the witch has over this one." Delia squirmed, and her green eyes shone bright with such intensity the light of the flames paled by comparison.

"See? Look what witchcraft has been done to this beast. Be gone with it." Leon shouted.

Estil took one look at the cat, and drew his arm back.

Natalsa emerged from the shadows and shouted at the top of her lungs. "No! Do no harm to mine, for I have done none to yours, Lord Estil." Natalsa walked forward purposefully, and the mob parted for fear of her. The crowds whispered her name, fearfully.

"This night your home was assaulted Estil, do you know that your own daughter was expelled from the home of your forebears and had to seek refuge from one you claim is evil?" Natalsa clasped her hands in front of her, in a gesture of peace.

"What do you mean, Natalsa?" Estil lowered the cat only the slightest of inches. Delia looked down at Natalsa, pleadingly.

"Someone has assaulted your home, and it burns as mine does. But from the number of corpses I've seen this evening, I doubt there is one other witch left in this city to be out of their senses enough to even stay within these limits. All the same, I gave your daughter Emmaline protection, and I encourage you to see to her welfare before ill comes to the girl." Natalsa looked all around her at the sneering faces of intoxicated villagers. "And if I may say, you are all worthy of reprimand. Where has your value of others gone?"

"None would dare stand against me, save the witches." Estil said, and eyed Natalsa with a respectful wariness."

"Save the witches." Natalsa shook her head. "Know that you have been wrong before, and you are surely wrong tonight. All I ask is that you spare my cat, for she means a great deal to me, surely as your daughter means to you."

Natalsa locked eyes with Estil, and for a moment, she believed he might see reason. He walked closer, with Delia in hand. "There is but one fate for a witch, now that your kind's crimes are known."

"What crimes? Present them that I may lay them to rest."

Natalsa realized what was going to happen seconds before it occurred. Before she could even attempt to make a leap towards Delia, Estil snapped Delia's neck, and the green light of her eyes extinguished in a snap.

Natalsa felt a part of her break, and her cry sobered up the crowds. They sensed her pain, and it rushed into their consciousness's and caused them to disperse. They began to flee under pretenses of kettles being on, or work in the morning, until only the most devout to Estil remained. "She was mine! And I loved her!" Natalsa clenched her hands into fists.

"Men, seize the witch, there is a pyre with her name scrawled on it." Estil said, and he dropped Delia unceremoniously to the dirt.

Natalsa turned to escape their outstretched hands, and she did not stop running until the moon was at the center of the night sky.

Natalsa couldn't have guessed how quickly the world would turn against her, and how quickly doors would slam in her face from people she once considered friends. "We can't associate with you; we have our lives to consider. Do you want us to burn with you?"

Natalsa's expression was grim, as she shook her head. "No, of course not Maralie. Take care."

With every mile that separated Natalsa from her former home, she grew a bit more at ease. Estil's influence could only spread so far, and she knew she would find someplace safe. She continued to walk for miles, and her feet began to hurt her so. She found she liked walking along the forest paths best, the wildlife kept her company.

She spent nights in haylofts, in churches, and in supply wagons - albeit often unbeknown to the owners of these locations. She ate what the orchards provided her, and whatever morsels of pity had been afforded her by those too bold to care about being seen with a witch.

She stared up at the moon on a particularly chilly evening, and saw that it had come to its full again, and she wondered in amazement that she had been on the roads for a full month since the purging of her home, Whittle's Bend. She bit into an apple and peered out over the land in front of her, the view a courtesy of the peak on which she sat.

She had reached seaside, and saw a village below that she had once visited when she was a girl. The place was called the Forks of Elkshead, and coincidentally, the furthest establishment from Whittle's Bend within the land. She had been turned away less and less, the further she ran. And as of late she had been receiving more and more generosity from merchants and passers-by. She believed that she was close to reaching a sanctuary. "Perhaps I can be here, and thrive."

She sighed, and drew patterns in the dirt with her long, curled fingers. She made a semicircle, and to its right she drew her grasping hand sigil. She chanted, and stared at the moon pleadingly. "Do not fail me tonight; tell me this is the right thing to do. Tell me I'm not making yet another mistake."

The dirt and the symbols upon it remained motionless, and she felt nothing flow down her head to her fingertips. It had been the same way since the night of the purging. The magic was being elusive, and she spat. "Of course, how selfish of me to get to know anything about this ordeal. Thank you, most generous spirits for your generosity tonight."

The winds surged and blew dust in her face, her sigil was displaced and she was left to endure a fit of sneezing. "Just once, I would like an answer not shrouded in mystery."

Natalsa entered the village as the sun rose behind her, and its warmth welcomed her. Her joints popped, stiff from sleeping on hard ground last night. The village had rows of houses, most made of a strange looking wood, some made of stone. They were close in proximity to the others, and there were a number of windows left open. The streets took on a combination of cobble, and dirt. But it was very inviting. Most of the village still slept curled in their beds, wrapped in wool and happy dreams. She would have given all the gold in her purse to be one of those people as of late. She felt her coin purse and had three gold pieces still left to her name, and walked through the marketplace determined to hang on to each one of those gold pieces. Unless there were warm pies, then she might have a few issues.

And issues there were. Natalsa could smell a hot, sugary fragrance filling the air, and she heard her stomach rumble. "Fine, you. Let's have something then." She wrapped her arms across her chest and followed her nose to the vendor.

The vendor had a modest stand, with broken axles and the counter itself was in need of refinishing. However, it was laden heavily with all varieties of pies and pastries. The delicious treats glistened as if the morning dew rested upon them, and Natalsa's jaw dropped. Scones. Pies. Turnovers. Sugar Loaves. "Burn me alive. I've reached the ever after anyway." She said in a voice a little above a whisper. She heard a laugh.

"Good morning, miss." The vendor chimed in, his black curling mustache tickling the tips of his ears. He was an older man, that is to say, older than she, but she couldn't think of him as more than five or ten years her senior. He rubbed his hands together near a small fire burning in a pit some distance from his stand. "If you find anything you dislike, let me know. It'll be one for the books. Otherwise, I'm here if you have questions. Just shout for Chubbs."

Natalsa smiled, something she had not done in weeks. A simple measure of this minor kindness had warmed her. "Oh, I'll do shouting you can be sure of that." She laughed, lightly, feeling good to have done so. "I've been on the road for quite some time, so I'm certain that rocks would be a delicacy at this point."

"Oh, that sounds like an unwelcome trip. I hope things get better." He offered her a Sugar Roll. "Here, try this and see if you like it. No sense wasting money if you think you might have better luck with rocks. I won't judge." He smiled.

She snickered, and tilted her head. "Are you sure? I'm not one for charity."

"This is no charity, I'm simply offering you a sample of what I have. And if you like it, you can buy another.

"Well, that seems fair." She took the Sugar Roll and bit into it. It was still warm, and the crystal sugar rested on her lips. Such sweetness!

His eyes seemed to brighten. "See? Much better than rocks."

"It tastes wonderful. I'd like to buy a sugar loaf this time." She handed over a coin and he nodded. "One moment, dear."

She received her change back from Chubbs and picked up her slice of sugar loaf.

"If you don't mind me saying so, you've got some unusual scars on your wrists. Looks like you've seen a bit of trouble. Do you bring any of it with you?"

She felt defensive. "No, no trouble comes with me. Any trouble I had is surely drinking away their consciousness even as we speak."

"That's good. Though, I wasn't judging. I was just curious. It looks like those scars came from something with six fingers. Certainly, not common, by any means."

"Would you like to know the truth? Or I can come up with a clever lie." She was offered a three-legged stool by Chubbs, and she sat after seeing his kind smile.

"Sit, talk with me. The mornings young and I love good stories."

"I came from a town called Whittle's Bend. It was where I grew up, and once I came of age, I protected the city from any manner of evil. Well, myself and my others."

"Your others you say? Are you a witch?" He asked, he shifted a bag of flour at his feet.

She felt nervous, and worried about what his reaction would be. But she wouldn't lie, to lie is to be afraid as far as she was concerned. "I am a witch, though it's complicated anymore. I have been stripped of my power."

"Ah. That happen often? We used to have a witch, she was lovely. I miss her very much." He said softly, looking at her.

"I'm sorry. Can I ask what happened?" Natalsa sunk her teeth into the soft sugar loaf, and whimpered.

He heaved a great sigh. "She too succumbed to the Malady."

Natalsa squinted. "The what?"

"You don't know of the Green Man's Malady?" He put his hands on his hips. "It's wrought this area with death for... I can't even remember. It's a local sickness, or so far as we know it is."

"So, what you are saying then, is that your last witch also died due to the Malady? And she could do nothing for it?"

Chubbs adjusted a pastry dish for the third time since she had been talking to him. "Elina was young, and showed such promise. She was always helping to keep us healthy, but then like all the others, or so I've heard, her magic failed her at the worst time." His great bulbous brown eyes seemed to mist up.

"Since then, we've made do with the potion stores she had supplied in her home. But those are dwindling."

"My wife, she also fell victim to it." He cleared his throat. She looked away, awkwardness filling her at the tear that fell down his face.

She frowned, her voice brittle. "I'm so sorry."

Natalsa dared to hope, and she pressed him further for information. "I am capable, even without my magic I trust you to know this on nothing more than my word. But I can mend, and I can help. More, I want to help, for I have wandered for too long."

He rubbed his stomach, and took a bite out of one of his wares. "You are welcome to try, her home stands vacant, and the fire of her chimney is long dead. I've not seen anyone else come this way claiming to be any sort of chemist or witch, or otherwise." He bit his lip. "Talk to Thomas first, if you truly must have approval. Thomas is our lawman, and he can be a tough sell, but he's always taken care of us here. He loves his village, and is not afraid to demonstrate that."

"I will have to find him." Her excited tone betrayed her calm demeanor. It would be nice to have haven once more.

"Can I ask for more information on your magic? You mentioned a complexity."

The wind began to kick up again, and she felt dust rush across her legs. "I, and everyone in my village, had our magic fail us. In every attempt that I've made to use it since, the powers are silent." She swallowed hard, as she thought of the burned bodies she had seen, of the nooses dangling in silent threat. "My other witches were burned, killed. All of us."

He gave her a wary look. "I thought you had said you brought no trouble with you."

"I have been on the road for a month, and have had nobody pursue me. I think they believe I am dead."

"Being dead does not mean you are gone. I've seen the dead do wicked things. Please, go on." He put a hand on her shoulder encouragingly.

"The lord of the city, Estil, rallied against us. He seemed convinced we had been having conversations and more with Demons, even though we have fought Desinder presences in this world for over five generations." She nervously scratched her wrists.

"Ah. The scars now make sense. It was the dark ones. What happened with those demons?"

"My dark one, its name was Kaltegys, and in our last battle we were banishing his forces back to their realm. He thought to try and take me along, as compensation. I was unwilling to indulge his wish, so he left his mark upon me. I am marked, and I am his." She trembled.

"You are his? I don't understand." He let go of her shoulder. "Does he claim you?"

She looked over at him, and her eyes were slits. "He claims my life; the scars are a warning to other demons that my heart will stop by his hands alone."

"Oh." His face reddened. "Oh. Well my goodness. I see."

"So, to the point, the lord of town had everyone turn against me, I believe alcohol was the main cause, but there has to be more. I watched many of those people in the town grow up, and all of them have nearly been treated by me for their ills. Something is not right."

"I would almost have to agree, given my lacking knowledge. But if you offended a demon so absolutely, you would be significantly blessed with power. And you say it has failed you?"

"I do not know why. But I am nearly certain that the event is directly tied to what I'm calling the purging."

Natalsa finished her sugar loaf and dabbed the edges of her mouth with her sleeve. Chubbs smiled, and handed her a spare cloth. "Dear, you can ask for things. Have this. If you want to stay here, you are going to be a neighbor, and we're never inhospitable."

"My apologies, Chubbs. It has been rough for me lately. Your kindness, and my luck, are alien to me after what I've endured."

He nodded. "Maybe one day I can sit for more of that story. It seems to be a harrowing adventure."

"It would unsettle the dead." She frowned.

"Well," he said, staring out at the rising sun. "Thomas is to the west, you'll hear him before you see him. He's unnaturally loud." Chubbs took a final look at Natalsa, and put an extra pastry in her hand. "I hope you are a good person, you seem to be. And I hope you can help our town, for we surely need it. Take this, and if you are capable, come visit me and let me know one way or the other."

She hesitantly accepted his gift, and had she been the person she was a month ago, she would have declined his charity. But a shrinking stomach could be one hell of a negotiator. "Thank you, Chubbs. I'll speak again with you, by the Sun & Moon, I shall."

"Get on then, the day's burning."

+ Chapter Two +

Natalsa **WALKED THE STREETS** of the village, and heard the day being born. Mothers yelled at their slumbering sons and daughters to rise for the day. A hammering of metal was sounding from down the street. Cows and goats were making a ruckus. Natalsa passed by several grain houses, and a lovely watermill turned at the border of the town. She walked happily, and safely, through the town and nodded in approval. There was a closed jewel shop, and fine clothing market, and most importantly, a library. She stopped outside of the library, and paused at the doors.

She tried to turn the handles of the doors, but they were yet to be unlocked it seemed. All the same, she inhaled deeply, and could taste the ages on her tongue, and the fragrance of old parchment filled her nostrils. "Oh yes. This place could be home. But I will need to be careful." She warned herself, and she placed a hand longingly on the door, vowing to return.

As she had been warned, she heard a loud voice shouting from behind her. She turned, and captured her first gaze of the man she presumed to be Thomas. He was dressed in a fine blue shirt, and comfortable looking slacks. He waved to people as he passed on, chirping "Good day!" and "Never better!" to anyone who smiled at him.

Natalsa grinned, he looked friendly enough. He had rosy cheeks and a light blonde head of hair. He was shorter than she, and that was uncommon in men she thought. All the same, she decided that maybe he could be a giant inside. Chubbs had certainly made him out to be so.

"Good morning, sir. Might I have a moment?" Natalsa hailed him, and he turned to face her.

His smile vanished and he tilted his head. "You may have two, but I confess I wasn't aware we had an outsider here. Tell me your name." He spoke differently now than he had just minutes prior. He was authoritarian now, and Natalsa could feel the steel in his voice. In the nodes of her neck she felt his own power resonate with her, and she knew a common soul. Though potentially dangerous, she determined at once that she wanted very much to be on this man's side. The magic was stirring, or maybe it was something else in her chest that was catching fire.

"You have my apologies, I was told to visit you concerning the need of a village witch. Chubbs sent me to you. I am Natalsa." She considered his searching hazel eyes. "Natalsa, of the Brim."

"Well, we do have need of a witch. Primarily, one a bit more concerned with healing the ills than causing chills. Would I be wasting our time by talking on this further?" He adjusted the collar on his shirt, and ran his hands through his thick beard.

"I believe I can definitely help you, and the village. I have healed and made concoctions in the past. However, my magic has been under stress lately." She watched him with scrutiny. She dared to hope, afraid that she would be let down, or sent away like she had been so many times prior.

"The purging, of course affects all of you. Yes, I've heard of it, and frankly I don't give a dog's clump of shit how you make people better. As long as you don't endanger my town, we can work in peace." His voice was coarse, with perfect emphasis.

She swallowed. "I hadn't realized the word of the purging had reached this far already. Perhaps I've been on the road for much longer than I had thought." She began to worry, worry that other rumors had reached this far.

"Those on the roads rarely hear news. I expect you are also unaware then of the new sect that has risen out of Ballisend? No?" He motioned for her to follow him. "They claim to be purified, and they claim that they have identified a branch of magic that is not so deeply trenched in darkness, as witchcraft sometimes has to be."

Natalsa walked with Thomas, and was intrigued. He spoke as if he understood Witchcraft on a deeper level than most of those who didn't practice. He was stuck in his ways, she presumed, as he was one of the first authorities that still showed regard for what is right versus what is dangerous. "I appreciate that you are of an enlightened mind, most people I've encountered, well some of them and a growing majority, have bought into the mentality that witches are evil, and too dangerous to be kept alive." She felt warmed. *This could be it.* She smiled, and he looked at her smiling as well. This caused her to grin foolishly.

"I have heard of many things coming from Estil's Seekers. Not all of them good. It seems to me as if under the cover of nightfall, he committed genocide with the help of a town full of drunks and fools." He led her past a cemetery that seemed far too empty if things were as bad here as Chubbs had led her to believe. He paused outside the white gates and stared at the rows of the dead.

"I know Estil, and I came from that village. I knew those people, and had grown there since I was little. But those who I saw that night were not my friends any longer. Though I saved their children, administered to their sick, and reaped with them during harvest, I was worthy of death." She tried to speak fairly, but could hear her own bitterness in her thin voice.

"Oh ho?" He looked taken aback. "You should have mentioned that sooner, Natalsa. Why did you delay?"

She pursed her lips, and covered her wrists instinctively. "My departure was not graceful, and I did not know what sort of man you are."

He put a hand on her shoulders and peered into her, and she wondered about him. "Do you want to see what kind of man I am?"

She liked feeling his hands on her, and she snapped her head to the side to snap out of her trance. "I will have to wait on that, Thomas - for anything you could show me now could be all for show."

"That is fair and wisely said. Tell me more of your departure? I think it holds bearing on our arrangement of you living here."

So, she told him of the last night in the village. They sat under a tree in the graveyard and watched as birds fluttered through the low hanging trees. Children ran past them and played without a care in the world. She heard a man singing.

"Your story is horrific, and I agree with you that it was insidious. It is no coincidence that so many of you were killed in such a large place. And now, from that very same place, a new source of power is being awoken."

"I am worried, but I am also content with simply existing, working on reconnecting with the magic that I can no longer fully control."

"Nobody ever comes to the Elks, you can live peacefully here, and conduct research, practice, refine, and of course, heal." He paused and looked at her. "I do not deem you a threat."

She wondered if he would have said that if she knew what Estil knew about her. His gaze was unsettling her, so she changed the subject. "What is this sickness you describe? This graveyard is too empty, but Chubbs mentioned a Green Man's Malady?"

He nodded, and heaved a sigh. "The Malady comes and goes, like seasons here. Its cause and cure have eluded us and our last witches for years now. We have appealed to other villages, but they are just as blind on the issue as we are."

Natalsa crossed her legs and wanted to hear more. "What is the Green Man's Malady, and where did it get such a name?"

"Waylan Greener was the first person to contract the Malady to our knowledge. He was our forest warden. It was his responsibility to patrol the forests surrounding our village and track changes in wildlife to ensure we were not at risk of an attack. There were all manner of wives' tales about the village. None of us paid them mind prior to him." He started to speak, but stopped himself.

Her heart raced at hearing this, for as long as she could remember she loved urban legends, tales of the dead, and the unknown. All of this drove her to discover her own power. "Tell me more. It seems so silly to pay no heed to legends, yet have a man who patrolled the forests."

"He was bored, and needed something to make him feel useful again. He had retired as he could no longer work in the construction of buildings. And he became a story teller to the children; I know they loved his stories. The forest inspired him, and he never found anything of course."

"Being with nature has that effect on people, much like listening to music inspires me. I love hearing the twang and pluck of strings." Natalsa thought of her mother who had first taught her to play, or attempted to. Natalsa eventually gave up trying to learn the instruments, but her mother never gave up trying to teach her so long as she drew breath. It was hard to believe she had been gone for five years this winter.

"I have things that do that to me, our own inner inspirational sprite." He smiled, and seemed to start over something. He beat on his chest quickly and cleared his throat. "Anyway, the change in him started gradually. He would go to bed much earlier, he would stop his stories mid-sentence and seem to forget where he was. He developed a cough first, and complained of blurry vision. Then he stopped telling stories at all. The kids all brought him get well treats, and Stick Men for good luck. Marie tried to treat him, she was the witch we had as this all began. Old, happy woman. The eternal optimist. But when she had completed her assessment of Waylan she came to me, and she wept. The next day she came to me with a vial of her own creation. She said, when the time came, and I would know when uh, that was, that I should use it on him. Might make things, less difficult in his final hours."

He swung his arms back and forth, fingers clenching and releasing as if he sought to strangle the air. "I didn't think that she had ever been wrong about any diagnosis, but she was wrong about his. The concoction didn't help at all, and there are moments of self-inspection that I wonder if I could have just ended his final screams with the business end of a hammer, and done him a greater kindness." His voice was low, and full of sadness.

Natalsa raised her eyebrow at him, and was struggling to make sure she had heard him correctly. He spoke so comfortably, that sentence, and she wondered how many times he had thought it in his head for it to sound so natural as handling business. "He was in such great pain?"

He looked aside uncomfortably. "He told me his being devoured from the stomach up, he could feel the biting traveling up his throat. He seemed to forget who he was at times, and kept calling out for help. I called for Marie, but nobody could find her. Nobody ever found her, for that matter. He developed a fever, and his skin became tinged green. With every case since, that's how we know the end is imminent. I listened to him, and prayed with him at the end. I prayed until his screams drove me insane, on they went and they became worse, incessant as a newborn, yet with none of the sympathy one gets from hearing them. It was a scream of such pain that it made you afraid that it would catch you, and make you have it next." He trembled, she noticed.

He took out a pipe, and tucked in a small pinch of tobacco. He lit and drew deeply, and closed his eyes for a minute. Natalsa watched him in silence, judging him.

"Yes, he was in such pain. It has claimed five lives in the last year and a half for our village. We've been lucky. Waylan, Alan, Sheila, Maggie, and most recently William. I want you to live here, regardless of those seeking you. But most importantly, I want you to try and find this root. Figure out why this thing exists, and put an end to it. If you do this, you will earn my very valuable friendship."

She laughed, something rare for her, as she again heard it and it reminded her of a streams trickling. "And why is your friendship so valuable to me?"

"Because, Natalsa of the Brim, you have no friends right now, or you wouldn't be on the road running from a town where you grew up." He exhaled, careful to direct the smoke away from her. He seemed about to say more, but inhaled his pipe instead.

"Is there something more you would have said? I don't want to cut you off and let that thought replay in your head as many times as the hammer scenario has." She waited, and felt the weight of the day on her. It would be nice to rest, and few were as deserving.

"Well, there was a thought I had." He smiled.

"And I expect you to share it."

"I was going to say, that should your old friends come a calling, they would wish they were on my list of friends. For all the love I show my friends, pity those who are at the opposite end. I once had a man tarred for trying to give jewelry to my wife."

She recoiled. "Well that might have been a little excessive, I'm sure a night in the jailhouse would have sufficed. Did he ever try and give her jewelry again?" She asked on an impulse.

"Oh, I'm sure he thought about it. It was kind of his job."

"What?"

"Well, he was trying to get me to buy what he gave my wife. It was quite expensive, in hindsight, I wish I had bought it prior to her passing. I mean to say he had a jewelry shop. And I do mean had." He scoffed, and looked up to the sky, and shook his head sadly. "We haven't had a jewel crafter come here since I ran him off."

Natalsa didn't understand at first, and then like waking from a dream, she clapped a hand to her chest and her usual trickling stream of a laugh must have had a broken dam somewhere along the line.

Estil had been at his ritual for hours the morning that would see his first real breakthrough. The broken body was before him, and minutes prior it had been dead; yet now there was a faint life beat in the cat. "Oh yes. This is excellent." He laughed dryly, and realized how long he had been at work in his dim underground work room.

He watched the cat's chest rise and fall, and willed it to do more. He began to pet the familiar, and softly scratch its head. He carefully opened one of its eyelids, and saw a white film over the eye. He was unable to get the cat to follow his finger as it traced symbols in the air before it. But it drew breath, alive once more.

The sound of creaking steps caused Estil to turn, and he saw Leon walking down the old wooden stairs. "Leon, what have I told you about entering unannounced?" He wiped his sweaty brow, and smelled himself, barely suppressing the gagging that could turn into far worse. "I have been down here too long, regardless, I am somewhat glad you are here. I've succeeded in ways that we've only dreamed of."

Leon came closer to him, the scars on his forearms standing out even in the low light of the room. "I am interested to see, Estil." Leon peered over the workbench and saw the cat breathing. "How marvelous. You are truly becoming exceptional with your new magic. I can hardly wait to be as proficient as you sir."

"Yet still dominance eludes me, and it is but a cat. But, progress, yes progress." Estil looked again at the cat and failed to see it breathing. He prodded the cat with his fingers, and felt nothing. He heaved a great sigh and closed his eyes.

"Faith, Estil. You have accomplished much today, come upstairs, take rest and eat." Leon said consolingly.

Estil was hesitant to heed his words, yet he did feel a renewed hunger now that it had been brought to his attention. "Tell me of our other progress, Leon." He cracked his knuckles. "I need to hear something good."

The two passed through the hallway of the forebears, well maintained portraits of former magistrates and rulers hung in honor. Estil walked past them, and puffed out his chest and swept his long hair back. He was continually reminded of how far he had to go to exceed their legacy.

"The news out of Hale Ridge has been confirmed, two more are dead to it. There is still no information on the cause."

"Damn." Estil bit his tongue and cursed the blister that he was enduring upon it. "What is that damn woman doing if not fixing this." He turned a corner and walked into the dining room. Food was waiting, and Estil sat down in the chair and had red wine poured for him.

"Mara has been spoken to on it this morning, I just left her chambers after having gave her *encouragement* to work harder."

"I'm eating you pig, do not turn my stomach." Estil chewed loudly.

"She claims she lacks the knowledge of how it operates. And how it chooses its victims."

"She speaks as if it is sentient." He said with wonder.

"It is a virus my lord, she is suggesting it has the potential to reach a level of plague."

"Enough." He bit into his potatoes and rolled them around his tongue.

"I apologize." Leon said, bowing to the knee.

"What is on Emmaline's agenda today, has she completed her studies?"

"Her teacher reports she is improving. Though she is hesitant to do the work once she leaves the chapel."

"She will never be the Seeker I need her to be if she is not dedicated."

"I could encourage her, also, Estil."

Estil felt himself grow hot, and looked up at Leon who was smirking.

Estil stood up and heard the chair crash against the wall behind him. He swung his fist backwards and brought it rushing towards Leon's chin. Leon cried out and fell backwards. Leon struggled to find leverage, but found only the table cloth, and with a crash he fell on his back and was soon covered in utensils and food.

"My apologies, Estil. I only meant it in jest. I thought you would understand." He sputtered, staring up at Estil with terror chiseled on his face.

"My assault was only in jest. I presumed you would understand, Leon." Estil said, and he turned from his adviser. "I'll be downstairs. Again, do not disturb me."

Estil closed the door behind him and descended the stairs. He tried to breathe to calm his heart, for he felt it hammering against his chest, and he hated the sound of blood rushing in his head. He could sense it. "I can hardly wait until he is needed no longer."

+ CHAPTER THREE +

NATALSA SETTLED HERSELF IN the small
home that once belonged to Elina, then Ixtarae before her, and prior
to her, Marie. All the witches graciously, or negligently, left behind
books, and she could hardly believe them doing so. As she
understood, Marie had fled the town, and Ixtarae had also fled the
town. She was uncertain about Elina, but it didn't seem to matter.
Strangely, two Grimoires remained, along with personal libraries.

Natalsa also found several collections of common herbs, old
garments, and ink sets. She piled all the old garments on the small
bed, and leapt into them smiling. She hadn't had an opportunity to
take any clothes from her old home, and had been wearing the same
outfit for far too long. Even in their somewhat tattered, and patched
states, they were boons to her.

After she changed her clothes, and bathed properly, she
began to read over Marie's journals. There were pages of the town's
history, and it turns out that Marie's mother was one of the original
settlers here, though she lacked any magical history. Though
interesting, Natalsa skipped to the portions of the Malady Entries,
and discovered to her dismay, that most of the common knowledge
was recorded there, at least, the information she had been told by
Thomas.

Yet, the remainder of the journal was filled with strange
symbols, presumably Marie's personal script, and it would take time
to discern, if it could be at all. Natalsa had her own code, of course,
every witch did. But there were no similarities that she could
decipher. Such was the shortcoming of any script.

Natalsa could see herself getting very comfortable here, and already she walked around the house adjusting it to her liking. There were doubts whispering to her, and she shushed them audibly. "There's no need to rush into things, I can stay here long enough to reclaim my magic, and then move on. It won't be long. It will just be for a few months." She lied.

The days in the Forks of Elkshead passed with ease, there was always enough to do, but she never felt overwhelmed. She began to develop relationships with the townsfolk, and nearly all of them welcomed her openly. Those that showed hesitation eventually broke down and welcomed her as one of their own.

Villagers began to call on her for medical treatment; there were broken bones, simple colds, scrapes and infections, but no further cases of the Malady presented itself. Natalsa looked for time to read over Marie's notes, but it was a slow process. She had managed to obtain a fair idea of what a few symbols meant, but could not determine how many weeks away she was from determining anything of consequence.

She was poring over such symbols one morning when she heard a knocking on her door. It was panicked and accompanied by words she could barely make out. Natalsa opened the door and saw a young woman whose face was red as a turnip. "I'm Penelope." She reached out and put her hands on Natalsa's shoulders. "And my very good friend Chubbs said you had an emergency."

Natalsa's eyes grew wide. "That *I* had an emergency? I have none that I can think of."

"Honey. It's clear to me you do." She walked past Natalsa and took a seat at her kitchen table, sitting quite comfortably with her feet propped up on a chair.

"Please come in." Natalsa said, hesitantly closing the door. *You had to get rid of the dagger, didn't you Natalsa?* She shook her head at herself. *All the crazies come out now you know that.*

"I see that you do not have any real friends here! And dear, that's what I'm good at. I'm here to be your friend. Me and my love, Guy, are in dire need of a new friend. Being friends with *nearly* everyone in the town is unacceptable!"

Natalsa laughed. "Am I all that's left to surrender to your erratic friendship?" Natalsa took a seat, and stared at the young girl.

"Yes. At my last count. And we can be such good friends. I bet you haven't ever had anyone to take you fishing. And we have the best fishing holes around here."

"I've never had much luck with catching fish. They say there are plenty of them, but my luck is poor."

"Come on." Penelope said, getting up quickly. "We're going fishing, and you're going to catch one!" She grabbed Natalsa by the hands and dragged her out the door despite Natalsa's refusals.

"It's too hot out; I'm much happier inside with my books!" Natalsa pleaded with her.

"Books will be there forever, but fish are fleeting!" Penelope said ushering Natalsa down to the coast. The hot sun warmed Natalsa's spirit, and the girl's fun nature reawaked a happiness in Natalsa that she hadn't known in some time. She did catch her first fish that day, and she thought of how much Delia would have enjoyed it. She missed her familiar, and longed for that sort of companion again. Yet here was Penelope, as carefree and socially energetic as she could like.

"Maybe I do need a friend." She said to herself, as Penelope cast her line into the ocean, whooping joyously as it instantly caught a fish. "Even if it is just a silly girl with a fishing pole."

Seasons passed, and when the grass began to pop up from the darkened soil, it took her mostly by surprise. She had called the Elks home for two years, and was amazed at how easy it was to let time slip. She attempted to restore her magic, and spoke the words. She spoke, and scribed, but no longer felt a pulse in her veins where the magic used to flow. She wondered what had been done to the magic that night of the purging. She also wondered if the townsfolk were right, and she was a charm to keep the Malady at bay.

Carefully she recalled how Leon had tried to bind her, and how her knife had probably saved her life, where her magic could no longer do so. He obviously believed she still had her magic, else he would have overpowered her. She knew there had to be a reason for the failure of her craft, and had she the opportunity to speak with other witches, she might have obtained a solution.

She began to hate the books in her home, those grimoires at least. They were reminders of her failure, and her lack of power. She brooded more and more frequently and found no other method of coping than taking care of the sick. Every time she spared someone injury, or sickness, it brought her joy. The joy the magic had brought her prior.

She pushed magic out of her life until the first hot day of spring arrived, hot and sticky. She had worked hard to establish herself in the Elks, and was respected as a quality healer.

But spring brought tradesmen, and more than tradesmen. For the first time, the spring brought Seekers. The Seekers bore the news of a new power that they were mastering, and they eventually passed through every village in the surrounding area. Until, eventually, they arrived in the Forks of Elkshead.

On that morning, Natalsa was walking through the streets of the village, her brown hair flowing freely in the breeze. Her vision was obscured therefore, when the first of the Seekers paraded through the village gates. Natalsa did not see them, she had other things on her mind.

So it was unfortunate when a certain Seeker saw her, and more, he recognized her. For he was born in Whittle's Bend, and he knew of a certain person to whom Natalsa's survival would prove to be of great interest.

His name was Tristan, and he still found Natalsa beautiful. He watched her move with interest. But more than his admiration of her beauty, the wound of his rejected affection burned after years. He began to seek a way to overpower her, and then eventually how to turn her in to Estil. That was of course, well after he had had his way with her as often as he pleased. After all, wounds only get better with multiple treatments.

Natalsa was on her way to visit Penelope, who had wormed her way into Natalsa's life like a stray cat. Penelope's husband, Guy, would still be working. It was good to have company, and Natalsa had run out of things to do at the chapel where she took care of the sick.

The people pressed in on her as she waded through them in the marketplace, she smelled fresh fish and smiled with her eyes briefly closed. She would no doubt return later and pick some up for herself and dinner. She neared the end of the marketplace when she felt a strong set of hands grab her from behind, and before she registered what was happening, a hand was over her mouth. She wasn't sure if she was being the object of a joke, but the knife she felt pressing into her back quickly told her all she needed to know. She heard the jabber and ruckus of the market as if it were all coming from so far away, there was buzzing in her ear, and she was struggling to catch up to what was actually happening to her.

She tried to turn around, but the person behind her spoke for the first time.

"Ah, ah, Nattie, we mustn't do that now. Keep walking."

She was pushed further down an abandoned alleyway, where cats and rats resided, but few others. She tried screaming, but he muffled her shouts with his hand. There were rotted crates, and putrid piles of excrement. Her stomach turned, and when she heard 'Nattie' she knew who was holding her. Until this moment, she'd had no reason to regret donating her dagger to Emmaline, but she felt its absence heavily now.

"Tristan, I expect you to knock this off at once and tell me what you are doing." She heard her voice tremble and wished she could command half the authority she once wielded. She heard him walk clumsily behind her, kicking away cats that rubbed against his legs from the sounds of insulted yowls.

"Didn't take you long to remember my name, I'm more than a little surprised." He chuckled gruffly. "Maybe I did mean a mite more to you than you had let on."

"No, you're still a vile human being worthy of all my maliciousness." She tried to slow her pace, but he pushed her forwards, and she fell on her knees. She recovered quickly, cursing the pain that coursed up her body and saw an open door. She rushed towards it and managed to get inside, but not before he followed. It was dark inside, and smelled of decay, and metal. The door closed with a slam of finality.

"You will do no evil to me, or I will see to it that you will spend the rest of your life regretting it." Natalsa spoke through clenched teeth. She felt around blindly for anything that might serve as defense, but couldn't find anything suitable. It was all so heavy, and she felt him getting closer.

"Silly woman. Haven't you heard the news? Because I have. I know better. You can no more hurt me than you can make this room shine like the sun. Not anymore. No not a one of you can. " He giggled and she heard something get dropped to the floor. She bumped into something solid, and revealed her location. She spat and made a rush to get to the other side of the room. It was very disorienting, and if she could only get her bearings she might still be able to get away.

"What do you know of my problem?" She desperately wished for more time, or divine intervention. She quickly prayed, and hoped it would be heard.

"Estil has told me things, things that he and Leon have done. Did you know that he has magic now too? Except his doesn't rely on dark devils or perverting nature. His is the pure. And, he has told me that no witch has been able to cast so much as a parlor trick since the night we made you flee Hale Ridge. So tell me, witchy girl, what magic is going to save you from me this time? Huh? You're gonna be mine, and then, I'm going to turn you over to Estil. He'll be quite interested to know that you are still alive and quite well, at least for the moment."

Natalsa had a sinking feeling in the pit of her stomach, and she was stunned by the revelation. She had had suspicions of such, of course, but to hear it so plainly and with perfect speech, made her weak in the knees. If the magic had been taken, and not lost, perhaps it could be restored.

Natalsa felt Tristan upon her in the moment it had taken her to reflect on her reality. His hot breath and rough lips latched onto her, like slime on a pearl. His hands paraded across her body, and she tried to resist him. She kicked, screamed, and when he touched her below her dress, she bit him.

He pushed her back forcefully and she collided with a stand of some sort, for there was a din of falling metal.

"Bitch! Whore bitch!" He cursed her and she heard him groaning. She made to rise silently but tripped over whatever had been knocked over.

She felt the wind rush out of her as his body collided with hers. He tore at her clothes, and she felt hot, sticky liquid drip onto her. She tasted blood, bitter and metallic on her lips. She also felt him struggling with his pants, and she reached down and took the only option within her reach. She grabbed, and twisted until his screams matched her own. Though his might have been more high pitched, and painful.

He managed to twist free of her grasp and she heard his heavy breathing. "You couldn't do this the easy way, could you whoresmaid?" She heard him struggling to get up.

Natalsa bent down, and crawled under a table, her eyes now adjusting to the darkness of the room. She saw him getting up, and looking around, trying to find her. She had to make the first move, and her eyes fell upon a metal rod. There were several lying on the floor, and she thanked fate for providing her this escape. She took one of the cold rods in her hands, and rose like a reaper.

She strode towards him, and breathed deeply. "You call me a whoresmaid, and a bitch. But you will never touch me again, you will never know my caress, or my kiss. You will know my fury however, and you are deserving."

She brought the rod down on his head, and she brought it down again. He grunted, and tried to wrest the rod from her grasp, but she would not be moved. She swung forcefully and brought the rod crashing into his neck, and he coughed terribly and uttered a scream. "You're dead, soon as I."

"No. You will never again." She summoned her rage, she drew in all the knowledge that she'd just been given, and knew that if she still possessed magic, this explosion would have had collateral damage. She took the rod, and plunged it into his chest with a strength she didn't know she possessed.

She waited until she was certain he wasn't moving, and then with all the will she had left, she rushed towards the walls to find the door. The walls were cold, and slimy. She ran into cobwebs which stuck to her face and hair, and she spat away the itching she felt on her lips. At last, she found the cold handle and turned it. Glorious light and fresh air rushed to her, and she looked back at the body she left behind. The room was cursed by his blood, and his desire, and his hatred. Life source had a way of corrupting or building places such as these, and she was certain this room would never again know anything good.

She stumbled into the market place and received concerned looks from nearly everyone in the street. She pressed past them, muttering about needing Thomas. She had to see Thomas. She walked past a group of men in white robes, and black crests on their chests. An E was emblazoned in a circle of red, resting within the crest. She had never seen any men such as them before, and presumed that Tristan appearing, and their appearance, were hardly coincidence. She was certain also, that Tristan wore garments such as these.

On she went, until at last she tracked down Thomas. She locked eyes with him and his bright smile faded into concern at once. He had his hand on his musket and he seemed to remember himself, and took his hand away.

"Natalsa, you look as if Hell paid you a visit. What on Earth happened? You have blood on your face, and you are red. So red." He eyed her, up and down and he pulled cobwebs from her hair.

"There was a man from my village here, you will find him dead down the alley near Decoursey's. He attempted to have me, and then he informed me he was going to turn me over to Estil. You should understand, I killed him. But ... " She realized what she'd just said, and what she had just done. She knew that shock must be causing all of this, the hurricane of her reality was she had just taken a life, and if she had only had her magic, she would have found any number of means by which to suppress an attacker. But because of Estil, and Leon, her magic had been stolen. She trembled.

If Tristan was truly his man, Estil's, when his murder was discovered, it would not take long for word to get around about who had done it. And Estil would hear. Then Estil would come.

Natalsa was afraid, and she fell upon Thomas' chest, weeping.

+ Chapter Four +

THE NEWS THAT NATALSA had slain one of the
Seekers spread like a plague in the village. Everyone was inventing
every sort of injury to get her attention, trying to pry details out of
her. She however only wanted the company of Guy & Penelope, and
occasionally when necessary, Thomas.

Penelope was a warm, quiet girl with black hair far too thin
for her age. And her heart was promised to Guy, a scribe who had a
gentle hand and was terribly soft spoken. Natalsa awoke to both of
them ministering to her, Penelope was redressing an injury on her
arm. She grimaced as her friend tended to her. "I'm not lying when I
say I'm fine Penny. You needn't spend your time here waiting for me
to slip into sickness."

"Well, you say that now, but I ain't going to have your
welfare bust on my watch. B'sides, Guy isn't home for long between
journeys. Plus, this place is cramped, I've been cleaning up a bit."

"You really shouldn't have." Natalsa said, swinging her legs
out over the bed and stretching timidly. Her muscles burned, and she
felt several hot spots on her skin that didn't reach well to the stretch.
She inhaled sharply, and lowered her arms gingerly.

"Thomas came by again. Were you awake the first time?"
She scrunched up her face and her large front teeth bit into her lower
lip. "I can't remember what he wanted the first visit. But the second
time he left you this, said it wasn't wise of you wandering the streets
unprotected after what you went through." Penelope slid her a long
slender box, wrapped in plain paper and white twine.

"Well, ain't you going to open it Natalsa?" She proffered the
package to her.

"I'm not in the mood for presents right yet. My heads still feels sloshy."

"Well goodness be, mind if I open it? I can't stand not knowing things. Specially not with a gift like this." She shook it, and then sniffed it. "I haven't a clue what's in it but I've been dying to know."

Natalsa waived her hand dismissively and walked into the pantry to get some fruits. "Go on then, entertain yourself." She said sitting on a bench and staring out a half circle window.

She watched as Penelope bit through the twine with her teeth and slid her fingers under the breaks in the paper. She slid bottom out of the box and gave a low gasp. "My word, Nattie, it's gorgeous."

Natalsa cringed. "Don't call me that anymore Penny. I can't bear the thought of it." She felt green around the edges, but walked over and looked at what was enclosed. Her eyes widened in disbelief.

Every witch receives a dagger after their dedication, or more commonly known, as their year and a day initiation into the craft. After giving hers to Emmaline, Natalsa had never replaced hers, not knowing a need to since she had stumbled upon the haven of the Forks of Elkshead. Yet here, in plain shimmering steel was another dagger. It had a glimmering black handle, from which a pointed blade extended. The edges were sharpened to a fine keenness. She picked it up, and held it in her hand. It was clearly of some value, she could discern as much from the craftsmanship.

"My Lady." Natalsa uttered to the gods affectionately. "Such a beauty."

"Natalsa, there's a card as well." Penny held it up.

Natalsa picked up the small square of scrawling text, and read:

Natalsa,

I know you would have used your own, had you one upon you.

Hoping that this one will serve you well, should the need present itself.

-Thomas

Again, Thomas was a point of fascination for her, and she wondered what she had done so far to earn his attentions. She had a thought, but swept it away in a dusty corner of her mind. She didn't have time for such ideas, they were idle, and rarely led to progression of anything that mattered. She had her object of affection, or she soon would again, she reasoned.

As she tucked the dagger into the hidden pocket of her sleeve, there was a pounding knock on her door. "Damn them." Penelope cursed, hiking up her dress as she stood and walked over to the door. She cracked the door open a sliver and peeked out. "I told you all before, she's asleep and is too ill for company."

There was muttering outside, and Natalsa strode forward, trying to hear more. She saw a gathering of three or four men, all in the Seekers robes she had seen them in prior.

"You'll simply have to try back later." Penelope said, as she began to shut the door.

However, Natalsa stopped her from doing so. She gave Penny a reassuring nod. "I've got this. I will not cower."

She opened the door fully, and stood facing the men. The tallest of them, a man of brown hair and a beastly set of forearms stared down at her. "There now, she's up now isn't she?" He said in a tone of voice that seemed at odds with his large frame.

"I am Natalsa. What do you need?"

"I'm Calvin, Official of the Seekers. We have been understanding up until now, but we will seek answers now. Will you keep us on your front door uninvited?"

Penny pulled on Natalsa's robes, and whispered her back inside. "We can wait for Thomas." She pleaded. "Or even Guy. We don't have to have them here." She sounded afraid.

Natalsa stepped forward, and closed the door behind her. "We will all stand outside, and be as outsiders together. What questions do you have, Calvin? Shall I tell you about how your man saw to have me raped, and handed over like a criminal?" She tapped her toes on the cool cobblestone underneath her, and felt peace flood her.

"What happened to you was not something we would have done, the order has specific rules about conduct. We will, however, need to write an official statement and provide it to Estil for when he questions why there are fewer men returning than he sent out."

Natalsa took a piece of charcoal out from her robes and tore off a scrap piece of blotched parchment. She drew her sigil upon it and handed it to Calvin. "You can give that to Estil, and I'm sure everything will be understood. However, do not waste your time returning here, I shall be long gone by the time the sun rises. And you can tell him Tristan informed me of everything. Tell him, I'll not be a flower soaking sun as I have been. Retribution comes." She spoke like she once did, back when the powers of earth were hers to command. It felt good, yet she knew she was empty. She hoped that she was fooling him, however. His men certainly looked weary.

But not so with Calvin. He took the sigil and put it into his robes. But thereafter he got quite close to her face, she could smell his oily skin and days old breath. "Tell me something, Natalsa. I've heard about you from Estil, and he spoke with a fearful reverence. But something doesn't make sense."

She grimaced, and remembered every hex she'd ever known. She desired nothing more than 30 seconds of power, that's all it would take. "Oh?"

"I find myself wondering why he's interested in finding you alive anyway, as if you were somehow valuable. Exquisite even."

"I have more value in my left foot than you do in all your body, I would say."

He spat in her face, and she felt the clingy, vile spittle hit her in her left eye. She reached up in alarm and began rubbing it as if to purge it out of her system.

"Come on, you pissers. We got what we came for. She's got nothing." Calvin said, and he lumbered off, his men close behind. He was about 30 yards away when he stopped, and turned around to face her. She was proudly standing cross armed in front of her house, daring him to come closer.

He laughed.

He knelt down and picked something up from the ground, and with a speed she'd not anticipated, he flung a rock towards her. She ducked, yet as the glass shattered she realized his true target was never her. Penelope's scream broke the moment's silence and clouds passed over the sun. "Bitch." He called, and walked away.

Natalsa rushed inside and saw Penelope wailing on the floor, pieces of glass were scattered all around her, and she clutched her eye with wracking sobs. "Natalsa, dear God it hurts, my soul it hurts!" She wept and Natalsa urged her hand away to look at the damage. Her eye was bloodied, and small fragments of glass surrounded her right eye. Bits of glass were embedded around her nose, and she sobbed. Tears mixed with blood and Natalsa was fire. She felt it all in her, yet had no direction for it. This was the stuff of powerful magic, and she had no way to send it outwards.

She ran for a cloth in the other room and dabbed water around her friend's eye. It was a senseless act of violence, and made Natalsa grip the cloth in anger as she dunked it into a bucket of water she kept in her kitchen. She administered to Penelope's injury.

She spent the next hour moving her friend to the bed, and once there, she ground up a local remedy she had discovered that would ease pain. An infusion of wrathroot and addlers tongue. She mixed it in with piping hot water and served it as a tea. "This will help you, Penny." She whispered, stroking the girl's hair out of her face as she sipped between sobs.

"I don't know if I can see, Natalsa. It hurts to open my eye."

"Then don't dear, if it hurts to do something cease it at once! We can worry about your vision, but right now you must be easy." Penelope struggled briefly, trying to move. Natalsa held her close and soothed her.

Natalsa sang her to sleep, which was fitful. Natalsa got up and took a look at her window, and placed a long cloth over it fastened by two nails. There she found vengeance waiting in her heart, and she wondered if it hadn't been there for months now. It was surely welcome.

Natalsa heard a knocking upon her door, and she turned to see Thomas at the window, staring at the broken panes. "Natalsa, Penelope, are you alright?"

"Come in, Thomas." Natalsa called, leaving Penelope's side for the first time since she had fallen asleep. There was an eye pad covering the right side of her face.

Thomas stared incredulously at the reversal within the house. "What has happened while I was away?" Thomas went to Penelope and looked at her critically.

"Estil's Seekers came to call again. I had words with their brute, Calvin, while Penelope watched from the window. I offended Calvin, in my arrogance, and as a result he threw a rock straight towards the window from which Penelope was watching." She paused to catch her breath which was suddenly short, and carried on. "She had glass shards embedded in her eye and skin, I'm not sure how much of her vision will be affected by it." She turned to her friend, whose chest rose and fell. "This is all my fault."

Thomas didn't say anything, but took a turn about the room, passing by the window. "They are just as malicious as I feared. And they are not welcome in this town any longer. I will handle them, but I want you to stay here with Penelope. Someone needs to watch her, and I'll send a courier to Guy. He needs to be back here right now. When my Sheila fell to the Malady, I was by her side. I know he'd want the same."

She frowned because it felt appropriate. These days, whenever the Malady was mentioned she felt guilty. She had hardly spent any time trying to figure out the cause and cure of it. "You needn't make any stand against them. It will not be worth the time after I've left."

He paused and turned to face her. "Left?" He shook his head incredulously. "I'm not sure you understand how this works. We do not succumb to fear or the demands of villains. This town has stood because of the strength of our will, and I will not have these bastards running in and scaring off my people. And regardless of what you've failed to do, you're part of this town. I do not hold it against you, the task is daunting."

She could have been slapped and felt better about it. She would have welcomed that at least, she knew how to deal with that sort of pain. "It's not that I don't want to help, there's so much to be learned."

"I have said it before, I do not blame you. You are on a timeline, and the next case will come for our village. It could strike any of us next, and I trust that when that happens you will be quite motivated. You have had other things to do, Natalsa. I understand. You have your objectives, and I have mine."

"I could leave."

"And I could let them take you and have anything I wanted from Estil's band. But there are degrees of righteousness, and I prefer to do what I know to be right. These 'purified' Seekers have shown me that they are nothing more than brigands. No. You are staying." He turned and left, the door closing behind him gently.

"He didn't raise his voice once, but my ears are ringing." She said to herself, in nothing more than a whisper. "I know I've been sloth." She wrung her hands together, and walked to Marie's notebooks. "I didn't start because I was afraid of not finishing. How am I supposed to figure this out, letter by letter, until it all makes sense? If I had magic, it would be the work of a few weeks, instead of months." She slid to her knees, with notebook in hand. From behind her, Penelope stirred in her sleep.

"Of course, if I were still Natalsa of the Brim, that entire scenario would have played differently. I could have prevented all of it. And rendered Calvin into fearful masses of man fat." She pursed her lips. "I've waited too long, and grown too complacent."

She withdrew the dagger Thomas had given her, and though she lacked the magic, she prayed the prayer for consecrating it. She opened a vein in her wrist and then dipped the blade into water. "Mighty forces of Earth, bless this blade of my blood, and may my essence be captured within. May it return to my flesh if the need is dire, and my days are spent. Bless & protect me on my journey as it begins anew. So I speak, so I will."

Natalsa rose up, and tucked the blade away, until it was needed.

Thomas had requested the assistance of a few laborers to move the wrapped body of Tristan out of the city in the bed of a wheelbarrow, and it had the desired effect on the Seekers.

"He is our dead." Calvin strode forward, hailing Thomas. "We must bury his body per our faith. If it pleases you, Lawman, let us do with him as we will."

Thomas smiled pleasantly and turned to face Calvin. "It would please me to have his corpse outside the limits of my village. I do not inter the bodies of rapists and villains here for any man's sake. You will find him outside, but you'd best hurry, the sun sets soon and the coyotes will be looking for ought to eat." He smiled dangerously, showing only the minimalist number of teeth. He wondered, could they sense his resistance, his desire to battle? It had been so long since he'd had a good tussle.

"Coyotes? Villains?" Calvin stared at him, appearing as if he were trying to discern if he had heard correctly.

Thomas stared at his features, square jaws and oversized teeth. His eyes were rocking on the side of a nose with a bridge longer than those spanning fjords. "Yes. Coyotes are typically hungry, they come from our forest. Along with all manner of other beasts, maybe you've heard our legends. And yes, I meant villains. After what I've heard and witnessed about *Estil's Seekers,* it is what I will be testifying of you. That your lot are naught but thieves of magic, and desperate harbingers of ill." Thomas said, taking great care to pull his cloak aside to reveal the holstered musket on his side. He rested his hand upon it, and his other hand upon a long sword.

"Now, perhaps I am but a simple lawman, and certainly no practitioner of your arts, but I would bet any unborn I have yet to father that I could at least cease the breathing of two of your men before you could finish an incantation. So, will you be leaving peacefully, and telling your lord of everything that you've witnessed in the Forks, or will you be adding bodies to the wheelbarrow? I will need to know so I can have my men prepare the burial cloths." Thomas watched carefully, feeling his heart flutter as a caged bird, and his feet felt light.

Calvin made no movement, nor did his lips part in the slightest for the longest time. A crowd had gathered around the two men to witness what was happening, such things simply did not happen often in the Forks. Mothers ushered their children away, and the pub emptied into the streets, men held their tankards of ale in their hands, making coarse comments on never really liking the Seekers anyway.

"Is that the one involved with Natalsa?" A child asked his mother, and she quickly pushed him out of the way, for Calvin looked around furiously.

"Now, now, remember Calvin." Thomas said, and he withdrew his sword this time. "That one is under my protection."

"You have substantial courage, Lawman, you realize what we could make happen here with our numbers." Calvin threatened, wiping his brow. He stepped closer to Thomas.

"I realize what you could make happen, but the advantage is on my side. For you have *no* idea what we could accomplish with ours. As I said, read into our legends. See what you find." Thomas said quite plainly, as he closed the distance between him and Calvin. "Now, I want you out. You have until the sun sets to get your men, get your lies, and get the distance between my town and your feet. I would not see your face around here again, if you like it intact." Thomas said, standing defiantly.

Calvin made a clicking sound with his tongue, and his fellows closed ranks until they were within inches of each other. "This won't end tonight. And my memory is long, dead man." Calvin turned and began to gather his men. He took his odor with him, Thomas sneered.

"I trust that it is." Thomas said, and he replaced his sword into its scabbard. He sang as he entered the pub and sat on the barstool. "Lemuel, I'd like a whiskey." He said to the gray haired and round faced barman. His smock was perpetually stained, and his waistband held rags of varying shades of yellow and brown.

"This one will be on me tonight Thomas. A show like that is not something I'd thought I'd get to see again in this life." The barkeep reached under the bar and pulled out an opaque bottle that was nearly full.

Thomas watched him pour the glass of whiskey. "Oh, I have a feeling the show has yet to even start old one. We're in for it, if Estil is anything better than his half-witted runners. They may command the 'purified' magics, but we have something better than that in this village."

"Oh, I know. I remember. But what if we fail?"

Thomas finished the whiskey, and felt his stomach warm. "The question is not if we fail, the question is, but what if we succeed?"

"That might be the whiskey talking." Lemuel smiled, taking a bit for himself of the whiskey. The whole rest of the world has turned from the old magic to this new breed. We are looked at as backwards hicks. I've heard stories from my brother."

"All stories have ends, like all stories have beginnings. Perhaps this is one or the other for us." Thomas drank from his glass, and felt its contents burn his throat.

Thomas asked for another drink, and sipped this one slowly, not wanting to get rowdy by any means, but simply wanting to repay the good graces of fate for their infusion of bravery he had just exemplified. He had acted brave, but parts of him were scared. He was glad to have Natalsa here, even without magic, he was certain they could rally a good defense.

Lemuel topped off Thomas's drink. "Would you like an old man's opinion?"

"If you see an old man, let me know." Thomas joked with him.

"Maybe you and that girl, the witch, can change our story." He smiled. "I'd like to see it."

Thomas grinned. "Maybe you will."

+ CHAPTER FIVE +

NATALSA MARKED ANOTHER DAY off on her calendar, as she had done for the last three weeks. Her fingers were stained green from grinding up herbs for such a long period. Her hair was frizzled in front of her eyes from being bent over a cauldron and burners. She had made her own grimoire again and her notes were all recorded within its pages in her neat handwriting. She was currently waiting on a rolling boil, and to occupy her time, she was deciphering the remainder of Marie's code. Food and sleep deprivation had fostered a great tenacity at unlocking Marie's notes.

Natalsa had made some progress on the recipe Marie had used in Waylan's treatment for his final hours. Marie had gone to Waylan and let blood, and with her magic she could determine it was something similar to an influenza sickness. The treatment she developed was comprised of Cally's Hood, a fauna that only grew in the neighboring forest to the village. Using that information, Natalsa had been working on a remedy based on everything she knew about sicknesses that operate that way. There was more to go, but she had been developing several racks of remedies now, not one like its forebear. She had so many to try, and each one documented, that at last she felt that she could relax slightly. If she could obtain a sample of blood of an affected person, she could proceed to testing further.

However, she looked at the cauldron boiling now, and feared the next part of her journey. To unlock her magic again would be daunting, and she wondered how she might go about such a thing. Everything she had thought had led to the same conclusion. There was only one person who knew what had truly been done to the witches, and that man was Estil. She heaved a sigh in frustration, and closed her grimoire. Taking a dipper, she withdrew the most recent concoction from the cauldron and poured it carefully into a phial.

Once she had placed the phial into a rack with all of the others, and made a careful note of which brew it was, she ran a hand through her hair. She put her black leather boots on and grabbed her cloak and satchel. She walked from the town and towards the heavy forest behind the town where Waylan so often tread. It had been part of her ritual these last weeks to spend as much free time in the forest as she could. Originally it had been for study, but now it was also for reflection. The forest was unusual in ways that were barely discernible unless you were paying strict attention.

Natalsa walked past squirrels, birds, and deer. She reached out and touched the head of a deer, and patted them gently. The first time she realized that nearly every animal in this forest was unafraid of humans made her wonder. It still caused her to tilt her head sometimes, and fill her with wonder. All except for one area of the forest, things were wonderfully tranquil. Natalsa felt her dagger in her sleeve, and was reassured as she began to walk through twisted tree limbs, and heavily armored thorn bushes.

The change in the forest was unnoticeable to anyone else, she was certain. Only those in which a perception of the supernatural had been trained would have noticed the difference. In a copse, thick with moss and an almost impenetrable row of trees, was a crumbling well. Since discovering it, Natalsa had felt drawn to this area, and she felt certain that somehow this was linked to everything concerning her quest for a cure. It was here that the Cally's Hood was most abundant. It was here that there were bears, or perhaps just one bear, and he was meaner looking than anything. Natalsa had seen him once up close, and the second time was from a distance.

She had to play dead the first time they had met, and while she was being sniffed over, the was overcome with the fumes of decay that seemed to come from the bear. After the bear had left her, she had to brush off several maggots from her clothes, and wondered about the bear. She had initially thought that perhaps the smell had come from remains left near the bears maw, but the second time changed that idea.

She had heard him coming from a distance, for he was not gentle when he trod through the forest near the well. Quickly she climbed a tree and hoped to remain still. She observed much that day, and got a better look at the bear. The bear was covered in black fur, save for his right hind leg, which was completely devoid of fur, and it had a gaping wound that still bled. It made her frown; for she knew the poor thing was in pain, it had to be from such an injury.

She had been taking to leaving behind honeycomb with a pain remedy sprinkled upon it. Just in case the bear happened upon it, and as the bear was commonly the only creature she saw inside this part of the forest, she trusted that it reached him. Today she heard him coming, and quickly sought refuge, but of course laying out the honeycomb first. She climbed up a tree, and waited.

Torga, or so she had named him, came about a few moments later. His gait was slow today, and she heard him crying out loudly, roaring for all his worth. Over and over he roared, but he found the honeycomb, and walked slowly over to it. Natalsa could see him well from her perch, and her jaw hung open as he came into view. His leg had healed, but was still without fur. The part that caused her such anxiety was that it was now unquestionably tinted green as ivy.

"This is a joke." She buried her face in her hands and listened to the animal's pained cries.

The cries stirred the sympathy within her to watch the bear gobble up his honeycomb, and only thereafter did his cries quiet down. It was clearly in a great deal of suffering. Its footsteps were slow, and labored by the rate of his breathing. Natalsa heaved a sigh, and waited to retreat to her home. It seemed she had her first patient who had succumbed to the Malady.

It was a quick journey to her house, but it took time to get the phials all sorted and safe for travel. She reached into her dry pantry for a jar of honey, and grabbed an overly large bowl. She hoped it would be enough by this point that the bear was trainable, that it would recognize the smell of honey near the well and come.

Torga was not in the copse when she returned, and she wasn't terribly surprised. "Nothing good is ever easy, is it?" She sighed, and set out her work. She inhaled the smell of the remedies, they had a sweet smell, unlike most other concoctions. She thought it had to be the local herbs.

"Of course knowing my dismal luck, the bear won't even come back today. That would be just like Torga. The oaf." She therefore took out five phials, and poured several drops of the would be remedies into the honey and stirred. She would then monitor immediate reactions & progress, presuming the creature survived.

"And let's just get these empty phials picked up." She paused to leave the honey near the well. Then she climbed up into her tree, stretched a hammock between two large branches and looked far down below. She drew her cowl around her head to block out the winds and began to write in her grimoire.

Torga came several hours later, near the point when she was nearly falling asleep with nothing to do. It was in the afternoon, but the heat was becoming a little much. She heard him first, clambering through the brush without grace. She watched him as he sniffed the bowl curiously, and pushed it with a mighty paw. The honey slowly poured out onto the grass, and the bear lapped it up. She looked down at him, and wasn't paying attention, and her grimoire slipped out of her grasp and fell towards the earth. The bear looked up as it fell a few feet in front of him, and he looked up to the canopy of trees. If he saw her, she wasn't sure of it. But he wandered off shortly after, slowly the forest filled with the sound of his pain.

Natalsa carefully climbed down and retrieved her grimoire. She set out more honey, and dripped the next five remedies into the sticky honey. She wasn't quite ready when she heard his pained roars fill the forest again. Torga was getting closer, and she didn't think she had time to get up the tree. She looked for cover all around, but found only the well. With abandon she looked down into its blackness and said a prayer. She extended her arms and legs and slowly climbed inside, careful to not move too quickly, lest she fall into the unknowable depths.

It was clear Torga was back, as she heard the bowl again being pushed around. She heard him huffing and roaring, but what was more, she heard something around her in the rocks to which she was hanging on. She was nearly sure that she was only imagining it, but the more she refused the thought, the more her hands burned. Particularly, the scars. Her scars burned, which was something they had not done since she had overcome the demon who gave them to her.

There was magic here, that was certain, and deep magic. Only that could explain her sweating palms, and burning wrists. Perhaps the legends of this village were a bit more believable now. She wondered if there was water here, and if it could be drawn. She was in the well for what felt like hours, but was surely only minutes. But her muscles ached from the exertion of staying put. When she felt she could no longer hold herself, she climbed up and prayed that Torga was gone. She peeked up out of the well, and peeked her head out. She was alone.

She climbed out of the well, and carefully inspected the center beam that held the rope to which a bucket was likely attached, with any luck at least. She jiggled the rope around, and felt a certain tug at the end, and hoped that meant the well was good. She began to hoist the rope back up the well, pulling as she went. She sat down her satchel of phials and honey and pulled with both hands, hoping to speed things up. She looked down, and could finally make out the image of the bucket, and from within water sloshed.

She brought the bucket to the surface, and looked into clear almost bubbly water. She sniffed it to see if she detected anything awry with it, but found nothing. Her wrists burned anew, and without realizing she was doing so, she dipped her wrists in the bucket. She immediately felt renewed and her wrists cooled. "Oh, oh it's here. This is goodness." She was so bliss filled that she didn't hear the return of Torga as he overturned her honey jar and spilled its contents out.

Only when the bear roared loudly behind her did she turn, shrieking. Torga turned up his snout and looked at the bucket of water, glistening on the shelf of the well. The bear ignored her completely and made a grunting sound at the bucket. When nothing happened, he looked at Natalsa. He repeated the grunt, and turned his focus to the water.

"This?" She held it out. "Is this what you want?" She asked, bemusedly.

She watched as the bear flicked out his tongue and began to drink loudly from the bucket until Natalsa was tilting the bucket back into its open mouth. Torga sniffed loudly and shook his head. He went back to the honey jar and pawed it listlessly. Finding nothing within, he looked up at Natalsa, and sighed.

She watched the bear wander off, and with his wandering, he took her wonder.

✛ CHAPTER SIX ✛

NATALSA RETURNED TO THE forest the next day, along with more honey and remedies. She set up near the well, and left a bowl of honey out for Torga, and she waited. She had worried overnight that the bear would die to the Malady, and if that was the case, she would know that at least ten of the remedies wouldn't work. Each time she awoke in the night she found herself hoping that the remedies did work, and though she tried to deny them, tears came. She hated to know that he was hurting, and that his roars were growing louder possibly.

She observed no other wildlife pass through the copse where the well was situated. She grew bored after a few hours, and went down to stir the honey. She explored further around the copse, and gathered some Cally's Hood for future recipes and experiments. She had thoughts of transplanting some to her personal garden in the back of her home. Without warning, she heard the bushes rustle behind her. She turned, and saw Torga approaching, his feet making swift progress towards her.

He walked right past, and went right to the honey and began dipping his paw into the bowl. She marveled at how disinterested in her he appeared; she'd have thought that she'd be the preferred meal. However, legend had it that every creature in the wood was docile. Perhaps the legend was true, and had no limits. She leaned against a tree and watched the big bear eat. His black fur looked so soft, and she moved carefully to get a look at his right side. She was scared to see if he was still tinted green.

The bear turned his massive head, and snorted. "Easy, fella. I'm just looking. I'm the honey lady, I'll be good." She spoke to him softly, and Torga went back to the honey. He snorted again, and dipped his paw into the golden sweetness.

"It can't be." She whispered, amazed at what she saw. She had gained sight of his right leg, and caught her breath. "By all the powers..." She swore. The green tint on his exposed skin was paling, and seemed to be retreating into his fur. The wound also, was turning lighter.

She smiled, and shook her head in disbelief. "I've done it, one of the ten was successful." She put down the remainder of her jar of honey, and opened the lid to let Torga have at it when he was done. She would need to return to check his progress, of course, but she certainly had enough work ahead of her now to fill the afternoon and evening. She backed away from him slowly and began to make her way back to The Forks.

It wasn't long before she heard a rustle of branches behind her, and she turned to see Torga not fifty paces behind, a splotch of honey sitting just out of the reach of his tongue. He let out a soft roar, and waited. She wasn't sure but maybe he wanted more. "There's no more honey, none until tomorrow. I'm sorry."

She returned to walking and kept hearing the follower. She smiled a little, and kept walking. After ten minutes of silence, from her at least, she turned to face him. He was quite close now, and his roar was slightly louder. He did not seem angry, but lifted his head higher to see her over the plant life. "I have no more honey, go home you silly bear." She ordered, and pointed back towards the well. Torga looked behind him, and then back at Natalsa.

She stood there as the bear walked towards her, snorting with every couple of steps. Soon he eyed her from a few feet away. He had dark gray eyes and he opened his mouth to roar softly. "God, your breath is really awful."

The bear nuzzled her and pushed her backwards. She caught herself, and laughed. "What? Do you really think you're following me home?"

The bear sat there waiting.

She would take a step back, and he would take a step. She would step, and so would he. On it went, until she, laughing, resigned herself to march home, with Torga close behind. "I really have no idea where I would even keep a creature of your size. My house is much too small for a bear, and the backyard has the garden. Stay out here, it's much nicer." She coaxed the bear.

He kept close behind, snorting all the way.

"Well, I'll let you stay the night, and after you see how dreadfully uncomfortable my back yard is, I'm certain you'll be eager to head back to your nice, eh, cave or whatever or wherever it is you sleep.

Natalsa had never felt like she held anyone's eyes, but as she walked back into The Forks, the villager's eyes were on her and her hairy companion. She supposed it was to be expected, not everyone walks around with a bear. Eventually, word of this had to have spread, for as she was nearing home, Thomas hailed her from down the street.

"Natalsa, what on earth are you doing?" He drew his musket and kept it at his side. His eyes grew wide as he approached, and his mouth was open wide. "By the heavens. That's a bear."

"Put that thing away, Thomas. He's not going to hurt you. But you are right, it is a bear. I had worried you might think it a rabbit."

"I'm certain he's harmless, or he'd have attacked my village by now. But you'll forgive me if I doubt his ability to stay calm. What is he doing here?" He looked at the bear, who was nearly as tall as he was, and he was on all fours currently. "Also, really? A rabbit? Come now."

"I think he's mine." Natalsa said, looking at the bear who gave no indication otherwise.

"Couldn't you get a cat?" He shrugged. "A pigeon? Something small?"

She frowned. "I had one of those. Had." She placed emphasis on the tense. "But this one, he's different. But Thomas, look at his leg, his right one."

Thomas did so, and he looked incredulous. "It has the Malady? A creature? That sort of thing is possible?"

"I don't think he has the Malady anymore. Thomas, when I first ran into him, yesterday, his entire leg was wounded and quite green. This is an improvement. He roared to the top of his lungs yesterday, and walked with such pained steps. I slipped him remedies, ten variants of remedies, and this is how he is acting today. Listen to him, no cries of anguish, easy steps, and completely docile. I think one of the ten potions cured him. And I daresay, if we look at his leg tomorrow, it will have even improved further."

"Well trust me, some congratulations is in order, but I can't act like there isn't a bear here. What do you plan on doing with him?"

She bit her lip, and reached out to the bear. He allowed her to pat his head, and his fur was just as soft as it looked. He inclined his head ever so slightly, and took a small sidestep towards her. It was clumsy, and almost knocked her over, but the bear was quite clear. "I think I'm going to keep him. I've named him Torga, and I think he's got more intelligence than any other wild animal I've ever encountered."

Thomas' expression was vacant. He blinked at her until it was too awkward to remain in silence.

"Are you still with me, Thomas?"

"I guess I am. I'll inform the town to not be alarmed." He scratched his beard and shook his head. "I didn't expect this. But onto the bigger issue, if you truly have found the remedy, then you have changed the outcome of any who would be susceptible to it. When next we get a human case, since apparently, animals can contract it, we will test it. If it is successful, then you have my friendship as promised."

"I thought I already had it." She was slightly hurt.

"Well, perhaps you have. But certainty can never go amiss." He reached out to touch Torga, who allowed him.

Thomas smiled. "Maybe he'll get it too. But you keep an eye on him."

"I figured I would let him ransack the bakery. Give Chubbs a good fright."

Thomas shook his head. "Don't make me regret giving you my permission."

"Come on Torga, let's see how you like Sugar Loaf."

Natalsa kept Torga in her back yard under an Oak tree. That was the only place the bear would curl up and rest. By the next morning his leg was completely missing the green tint, and even the wound was nearly gone. Natalsa wondered if fur would soon cover it again, she so hoped that it did. Natalsa caught him some trout from the river around lunchtime, and soon honey was just an afternoon dessert. Penelope also had a habit of bringing him fishes.

All the children of The Forks came to visit and befriend the bear, and Torga never showed any sign of hostility. People loved to talk about the Bear who came to stay, and soon he was something of a local legend. That Natalsa had apparently found a cure for the Malady also spread quickly, and it wasn't long before she received word that several families were attempting to make the journey to the Forks of Elkshead to test her remedy.

The moment of truth was fast approaching for her, and she made as many brews of the original ten remedies as she could. She was up late into the night and looked terrible by the next morning, for the work was tedious and had to be precise. Chemistry always had to be exact, otherwise who knew what the side effects could be.

It was around midmorning when she eventually passed out with her head on her workbench. She didn't hear any of the knocks upon her door, or at least, they didn't wake her. Her dreams were filled with summons from Guy and Penelope. She dreamed of Torga bounding through the woods, allowing her to ride on his back. She dreamed of friendship with Thomas, and perhaps a bit more than friendship. How much more, she wouldn't get to know in that dream. Dreams always have a way of ending just when they're getting good. She was awoken at once by the shout of Thomas banging on her door with all his might.

"Natalsa, open up! Estil himself has come to the village limits!"

She arose from her workbench, and was perfectly awake. She turned to her door, and made sure her dagger was secured in her robes.

"You can't be serious." As she opened the door, Thomas gave her an awkward hug.

"What was that for?" She asked, blushing.

"You seemed nervous." He said, somewhat out of breath.

"That was me being calm, pray you never see me nervous." She broke the embrace, against her own wishes.

"Right. Sorry. But he's here. He is not alone."

"Let's go." She stepped past him.

"Just like that? No plan, no anything?" He tried grabbing her by the arm. "We should have some idea of a backup plan in case things get nasty."

"I'm sorry, do I not have your protection? I would have thought the two of us could handle an evil man set on my destruction."

Blushing himself, Thomas nodded. "Fine. But I'll do the talking."

She was willing to let him labor under that delusion.

+ Chapter Seven +

NATALSA STOOD AT THE back of the crowd and peered over the heads of her neighbors. Torga was at her side, and rubbed his head against his shoulder with his head. Some of the children looked at her curiously, but she just smiled. She could see a little, but wanted to see more. She inched her way forwards, Torga stayed close by. His attachment to her was astounding, but she had already decided he was hers, the next familiar. By the light of the moon she had performed the ritual, and hoped for the blessings to carry.

A booming voice was heard over the scattered conversation of the crowd. "Natalsa of the Brim, I demand an audience." The voice was magically amplified, and she knew it was Estil. He had shown no magical ability all his life, and yet here he was, using it. The crowd parted quickly as she moved forward, and she saw Thomas rush to the front of the crowd, arms crossed.

"Estil." Natalsa said quietly, yet she was heard. She put her hand on Torga, and he plopped on his bottom with his rear paws extended forwards. "How ironic, the man who chased me from Hale Ridge for magic, commanding it with apparent ease. One wonders how the village received you when I was chased away for the same crimes."

He shrugged, his supple purple robe rippled in the wind of the breeze. "I am not here to peel away scabs, I am here to simply make a proposition to you. I have a tent setup nearby, some distance away, not too far." Estil winked at Thomas. "So that you may still feel safe. Post a guard outside, and when you have heard me out, you may act and leave."

"And why should I help you?" She tilted her head. Many behind her whispered their agreement.

"Because I know that you aren't the type of person to let another human being suffer. Come now, everyone here knows of your goodness. Look at their faces, so clearly well fed and cared for. Look at you, and your..." he swallowed, his Adam's apple rising up his throat. "Pet."

Whether anyone recognized the threat in his words, she was unsure. But she heard them. "I will go with you, but I want Thomas at my side. My *pet* obeys him enough to not do anything if I'm gone too long." She caught Thomas' eyes, and he nodded.

"The rest of you," she said, indicating to Estil's men. "Where will they be?"

"With me." Estil smiled.

"Then I want your most valuable man left here, to be our leverage should anything go wrong." Thomas ordered.

Estil smiled, and held up his hands innocently. "There is no sabotage planned here today, no treachery, unless you bring it with you of course." Estil nodded to his right, and it was only then that Natalsa recognized Leon. He looked grander somehow, his face brighter than she had last seen it. Perhaps it was his flowing garments, or his new staff.

"But of course." She whispered, burying her hand in Torga's fur.

Leon eyed her, and smiled as if he was the most innocent man who walked. As he passed Natalsa he dropped an infusion of Sage dabbed with crushed ivory. She knew what it was, and what it meant. Those were the methods used to bind witches, and inhibit their powers. But Leon was not clumsy, he dropped them intentionally, knowing that she held no power.

"Good afternoon, Natalsa." He said pleasantly, loud enough for villagers to hear him.

She held her tongue, and walked next to Thomas, Torga close behind.

"I don't trust them, and neither should you." She whispered to Thomas.

"I thought I was going to do the talking." He elbowed her sides with a smile.

The tent was grand, and clearly designed for periods when one would stay in place for a while. She wondered how long Estil had been here if he was staying in such a well-designed rest spot. Estil walked in front of them, and opened the tent for both to see. "There now, see? Completely empty, minus my dress and bed. You needn't worry." He gave a grin, and she noticed his teeth were a vibrant white.

Thomas stepped forward, but Estil held up a hand gently. "I will want to speak with her privately, but you are welcome to stand outside should it make you feel better."

"And let you alone with her?" Thomas scoffed.

"Dear Sir," he spoke silkily. "What would I do with her? Dress her in my garb against her will? Make her prepare my bed for turning in?" He laughed dryly. Thomas stepped forward as if preparing to escort her, but she placed her hand on his chest.

"It's fine, Thomas." Natalsa spoke tonelessly. "I will be alright. And there's no time like the *present*." She looked at him quickly, hoping he caught and understood her meaning.

"Torga," she said, looking at him in his great big eyes. "I'll be right inside, listen to Thomas." The bear looked at her, and cast his glance to Thomas. He snorted and sat down loudly.

Once the mouth of the tent fell close behind them, Estil began to speak.

"I will not pretend that I was not displeased to know of your survival." He said slowly, keeping his eyes on her. "I was even more displeased to know that you killed Tristan. I could have had the trade lines cut off to here, you know that, and I could have had this entire village razed by fire. However, I am quite glad I have not done so."

Natalsa surveyed him, watching his rising and falling chest, the sweat on his forehead, and the way he walked. She made sure to stay out of leaping distance, and hoped that it would buy her time should anything happen. "I will not pretend to be pleased to see you then, and I will state that I am even more displeased at the fact that you clearly come to me seeking assistance, when you have played me so ill."

"Oh, Natalsa. I hope you are not determined to hate me. Though, I know you have every right to." He held up his hands in a form of surrender.

"You stole what was mine, what belonged to my people, and you then insidiously gave birth to a faction of followers whose intentions seem far more sinister than demons."

"Well, though I trust you are the subject expert on demons, I will not allow you to vilify my order. We attest that we are using magic as it was designed, you can disagree with me if you want but —"

"I disagree," she scoffed as she interrupted him, "on the premise that it was told to me that you stole the magic from us, and I will let you know I have made measures to get it back. You know what will happen when that day comes."

"Oh, how have we come to be thus? I would like so much to put everything that was in the past behind us, I will even give you your magic back. I have no further need of it. All that I ask is one simple favor. Magi, to Magi." He smiled.

She watched him extend his arms, as if to embrace, and she took a step back. "Thief to Witch, get it right. I am here to listen. Be on with it."

His shoulders slumped, but he opened his mouth. "I have a friend who has fallen quite ill. He has the Malady, and you and I both now know why I've come, and why I was glad I didn't have you killed. You clever witch." He smiled.

"You want the remedy." She smiled.

"I *need* the remedy. He has been like a son to me, and in a few months' time, he *will* be a son to me. He is betrothed to Emmaline."

Natalsa felt her resolve shake at the mention of the girl. "How does she feel about this? They are betrothed. But tell me of her opinion."

"She loves him dearly, and they are set to go on a trip to the Islands of Alevaden. She has been struck mentally by this, and has not left his side for days. When I left swiftly last night as his skin took the green tint, he had already screamed himself hoarse."

She caught his body move unexpectedly, but was surprised to see him kneel before her. "Please, for the sake of their love, if not for the sake of your future and mine, and our differing views, save the boy."

Natalsa did not know what to say, but she remembered the girl. She knew the dagger she had been given would ward off evil, so surely the boy to whom she was engaged was worthy of being saved. "If I agree to this, what becomes of us?"

Estil rose and had a glimmer of hope in his eyes. "Why, if this is the beginning of a renewed kinship between us, I will restore your magic to you as soon as he is healthy again. If your bear is any indication that should be within a few days' time. I will return, with Emmaline, and she will want to thank you. Once she has done so, I will perform the ritual that will restore your magic."

"I don't just want it returned to me. Your son-to-be clearly means a lot to not only you, but Emmaline. I something just as dear to me. I want the magic restored to all witches, and amnesty given to this witch hunt you've led against us."

He hesitated, but then spoke slowly. "Of course, I will give you that, of course. But more, I will include you in some of the magic I have been performing, in the hope that you will take a keen interest in it, and perhaps help me to perfect it."

It was almost too much. Her heart was pleading with her to be cautious. "Why did you lead the purging? The man you were then, and the man you seem to be now, they're too dissimilar. I feel as if you are making a fool of me yet again, and I should leave." She said, listening to the voice of reason in her mind.

"I led the purging at the instruction of a fool, whom I thought I could trust. He planted lies in my mind and since I have seen the fruit of his labor, I have had him killed. Please, Natalsa, believe me. I have seen too much death, and the Malady grows ever stronger. We must confirm that it works. What better cause than for love?"

He walked close to her, and held out a hand. She eyed him warily. "You and I could make the world feel no more pain, we could sweep everyone up in our capable strong, and scarred," he nodded to her, "arms, and show them a world without suffering."

She considered his eyes, he was quite close now, and she could make out the wrinkles around his eyes, and the signs of worry were etched onto his face. "You killed a man, and you want me to trust you?" She saw him take a hand, and touch one of her fly away strands of hair. She shivered, and stayed quite still.

"Love can cure ails, this world needs love. This girl needs love. This world needs love." He whispered, and she saw his lips coming close. "Love." He whispered, as his lips touched hers, and she felt hers reach out for his.

When Natalsa had left the tent, the sun had moved substantially. The time she spent inside must have been far greater than she realized. Thomas came towards her, and Torga got up from his spot near a shady tree. "Natalsa, thank God I was getting impatient." Thomas said, gently touching her arm. "And a bit worried. Is all well?"

She looked up at Thomas and nodded. "Everything is fine. Estil and I have reached an arrangement that will be mutually beneficial to our village as well as his. And in return, I get my magic returned to me."

"Wait, what? Just like that?" He looked at her suspiciously. "Are you alright?"

She slowed her pace to allow him to keep up. "Yes, he was very forward with what he wanted." She felt hot under her robes.

"Which is?" Thomas inquired, as they walked together, with the big bear trailing behind.

"He wanted me to cure his daughter's betrothed as I have cured Torga. Once he is well, he will return to The Forks and make right on his end of the bargain."

"And you trust him to adhere to that? Why?"

Natalsa had to choose her reasoning quite carefully, and she kept her eyes away from Thomas. She still wasn't clear how everything in the tent had transpired. "He makes requests out of love, and I believe that maybe he deserves a chance."

"Natalsa you're not making sense. This man murdered so many of your friends, and your people."

"I am aware of what he did, Thomas. Thank you for being concerned, but I am choosing to give him the benefit of the doubt. Should he make a fool of me, I shall handle him with no hesitation."

He put his hand on her back, and she closed her eyes. She started to walk a little faster, and hoped that would be enough to keep him off her. "I'm going to give him the remedy combinations I have and then with luck I will never have to see him again. I am doing this more for his daughter than I am him." She frowned. "She is a sweet girl, and doesn't deserve to know loss so early. She already lost her mother at a young age, I would not have her lose her love as well."

"Well, if a young woman is involved, I can understand your compassion a bit more." His hand slipped from her back, and she breathed a small sigh of relief.

They continued in silence until they returned to town. Leon was standing just outside watching them approach. Natalsa looked at him, and saw him smile sweetly at her. She managed not to vomit, knowing that Estil was sincerely trying to turn his life around. "Good day, Leon." Natalsa said. "I will be right back with the remedies."

"Very good, Natalsa." He bowed.

When she returned a few minutes later with ten different vials he was still smiling. "Take these to Estil, have him administer each of the ten remedies. Progress will be observed almost immediately. Hurry now, he's waiting on you to come."

Leon tucked away the vials in his robes. "Well, he's waiting certainly." He leaned in close, and smiled. "But I think you and I both know coming is not something he needs waiting on anymore, is it?" He jabbed her playfully in the ribs.

She looked at him, with repulsion on her face. "Keep your mind out of my memories. That is no business of yours."

"My apologies, Natalsa. Thank you for your village's hospitality." He turned to take his leave.

She watched him go, and though she could trust Estil, she would never trust Leon. She was certain that sometime in the near future, she would need to do something concerning him. She shook her head, hoping it would shake him out of her mind, if any part of him still lingered.

+ CHAPTER EIGHT +

NATALSA BROODED IN HER bedroom, staring down at her body. Hours later she was uncertain how to feel about what had happened in the tent. He had been charming, and she was almost certain she had been under no spell. He had been married once, so surely he knew how to be romantic, how to touch a woman. She though again to Thomas touching her back after she left, and how she had felt guilty. Yet, she oughtn't feel guilty, she was nobody's property but her own. She had been willing, to her surprise even, but she was by no mean forced to do anything she hadn't wanted to.

"It was standard, the experience, nothing world shaking, but not terrible. And we had made a pact, and it was not so uncommon for witches to seal arrangements with a kiss, and sometimes more. I didn't do anything wrong." She reassured herself. She cracked her knuckles, and stretched around trying to pop her back. If she meant anything to Thomas, it was not her responsibility to act first. She had nothing to feel bad over, so why couldn't she be at ease?

The boy would soon have his medicine, and Emmaline would have her happiness and wedding day. She could almost taste the tingle on her tongue again, of the magic, and felt anxious over being herself once more. She thought deeply on the Seekers and how they performed magic, or rather, how she believed they conducted magic.

To her understanding, magic was magic. It all came from the earth and there was no pure form, it simply *was*. The difference she could see was how it was spun to the villagers, if they called it divine magic, then that's what they believed it to be. Outsiders, unless they studied, knew no different. And since anyone could learn magic, all Estil had to do was find willing participants to buy into his idea of purity.

She wondered how many witches of her order remained, and how their order might be rebuilt. There was so much to think about, and so little light left in the day. With a heavy head, she put her head on her pillow and sunk into the softness of the bed.

Estil approached Anthony's bedside and felt his forehead, it was so hot. His sheets felt damp, and there was an odor of urine and sweat. It was like a greenhouse in the bedroom, and he seemed to give off nothing but heat. His skin was near painted green and his breathing was shallow. Emmaline was passed out next to his bedside, her head resting on her arms.

"Emma, come by love." He patted his daughter on her head and gave her a kiss. He lifted her up after she did not stir, and cradled her in his arms as he had done when she was a baby. He knew she hadn't slept much lately, and was glad that at least exhaustion claimed her. He placed her in her bed and covered her with her blankets before leaving the room.

He took the vials that Natalsa had provided and went into Anthony's room to administer the remedies. He locked the door so as to not be disturbed, and began the task of dropping the concoctions down his throat.

For hours he sat near the boy after the medicine was given. He watched for signs of relief, for signs of improvement. Often, he stroked the young man's brown hair, and placed cool damp rags on his forehead to comfort him. He recounted stories of his youth, and of the first time he had lain eyes on Emmaline's mother. Though he knew the boy wasn't hearing him, it comforted Estil to do so. He held Anthony's hands as his screams woke him from his slumber.

"It's alright, dear boy. You have the cure, you will soon be fine. You and Emmaline will have your day, and my daughter will be happy. You both will be, be still and rest."

Estil didn't remember falling asleep, but he dreamed of Natalsa and the time they had spent together. He had treated her so badly, yet he felt such closeness to her when they were talking. Perhaps all could be forgiven, and a peace could be had. His dreams shifted to a cacophony of demons, summoned by Natalsa, like the one she had summoned all those years ago.

The screaming became so intense, it made him realize that he wasn't dreaming the screams. He awoke to find Anthony convulsing on the floor next to him. "Anthony!" Estil shouted, as he put his hands on the boy's head to stop it shaking so violently. This did little to help him, as Anthony still reacted violently.

"Leon!" Estil called out. Leon would come, he would know what was happening, how to help. Estil gasped as Anthony's temperature started to increase, his head was so hot. "Leon!" Estil shouted again. "Dammit man, where are you when I need you?" Anthony's head swung violently back and forth as his eyes burned to red blotches, and he cried for Emmaline.

Estil himself tried calling for Leon once more, before giving up on him. "The damn fool. Curse his face!" Estil looked about for another of the remedies, and emptied the contents that remained into Anthony's mouth, which showed that his gums were bleeding terribly. "Stay with me, Anthony. We can't lose you. Emmaline can't lose you. Help!" He shouted again, willing that anyone would come to his aid. He tried to think of a spell, but he was under such strain that all words of magic escaped him. "Spirits why aren't you here when I need you?"

Because you have murdered our chosen. He thought he heard this reprimand in the back of his head, but brushed it away. "Somebody help me!"

"Emmaline!" Anthony screamed in agony, his eyes opening as wide as they could. "Emma –"

He stopped screaming all too suddenly, and his form became immobile.

Estil's mouth was agape, and his eyes frozen on the corpse of his would-be son-in-law. He placed his hand on the boy, and shook him as if to wake him from slumber. But the boy way gone, and the witch's treachery entered his heart. "She tricked me, she played me like a fool." He ran his hands through his hair, and his daughter's face filled his mind.

"I must tell her tomorrow." He slammed his fists into his legs. "Tomorrow, I will have to destroy my daughter's happiness."

He slammed his fists against the stone walls and cursed at the top of his lungs. He opened the door, and regardless of the hour he approached Leon's quarters. "Leon! Leon get out here now." He paced the hall, fury bubbling inside him until he felt it would explode.

"The hour, Estil. What is the matter?" Leon said sleepily.

"It is the witch. She has betrayed us. Anthony is dead." He said through his own rage.

Leon knelt and held his hands in a prayer. "This is awful. Emmaline will surely be devastated. What would you have me do?" He asked solicitously, with a certain grin hiding in his frown.

Estil sneered at the man kneeling before him. "Cut off the supply lines. I will make *her* downfall my only goal. She has toyed with me and I will not suffer that she should live any longer than she has now. Tell everyone what she has done, how she abhors the wishes of two young adults in love. Tell them all how she has destroyed adoration, and rendered the future of my daughter to ashes. Tell them. And make ready. The witch will pay for her treachery."

Estil went to a window and stared out at the moon, and when he thought himself alone, he smiled at the thought of ending Natalsa. He felt his emotions surge through him, not sure what he should be feeling. One moment, he felt love. The next, rage so black it could consume his soul. Maybe it already had. He struggled to remember a time where he last felt normal, and he grew quite tired. Unusually tired, and he retired to his chambers.

Emmaline had found her solution to not feeling normal, and it had come in the form of Anthony Coalfist. His family wasn't wealthy, but they abhorred violence and loved much. He was supposed to have been her eternity, and now she put on colors of mourning and prepared for his internment.

She took one last look in the pocket mirror she kept for when she had to be sure she looked okay, and she supposed her cheeks weren't too red. She carefully slid her good luck charm into the special boot slot she had crafted, the old blade the witch had given her on the night of the Purging. Nobody in the town recalled that night very well, they just remembered what came after. The denouncement of Witchery, and the rise of the Seekers. But Emmaline remembered much more than others and she cherished her gift of recollection.

She remembered the witches being scared, she remembered a man named Leon not existing before the Purging, and she remembered the woman who gave her the knife showing her where to hide when her family had come under attack. She kept Natalsa's dagger out of strictest respect for her, and she knew it was an artifact of power. She could feel it still, a feeling of sanctuary, and warding. Therefore, she never left home without it.

They gathered around the grave, his family and his friends. And she stood next to her father, clutching his hand and trying her best not to give into the tears that tugged at her eyelids. The sky did not seem to mourn Anthony's passing, for it wore the brightest blue and fluffiest crown of clouds. She heard the twitter of birds and envied their song, for they did not have the ability to understand this level of grief.

After the funeral, Emmaline rode back to her home in a carriage with her father. No sooner had the doors closed and the horses began to trot, she breached conversation again with her father.

"I appreciate you trying to save him, Papa. But I have considered your story, and I do not believe all that I have heard. Is it possible you have overlooked anything?" She clasped her hands in her lap and stared at his thinning hairline, and shaking hands. How long had it been since he had slept?

He parted his lips slowly and reached out to touch her leg. "Emma, I am capable of mistakes, but I see no detail that has been overlooked. I know you were hoping too that she would help us, and I listened to you, didn't I?"

"You did after I had nearly lost my voice from pressing you with requests. I do not think she has it in her to treat us so poorly, it is not the Natalsa I have heard such legends of."

"People can change dear, especially when there are battles to be fought for survival. She sought to hurt us, and cause you harm. That or she simply did not believe the remedy was for Anthony." He tsked.

"No, I refuse to believe that."

"Try and have faith my love, the world will not always be black roses and heartache."

She dabbed a tear that started down her cheek. "You've never gotten over mother dying. What if I end up like you?" She covered her mouth as soon as the words were out. "Oh, papa! I did not mean that the way it sounded. Please do not be upset."

She saw him close his eyes and nod his head. "You are stronger than I am, and you are far better looking than I am. You will find a way to live past your grief, it's what Anthony would have wanted."

She pressed her lips together. "I don't think Anthony would persecute her further by placing an embargo on The Forks of Elkshead. And all of those innocent people."

"People who cohort with a witch? One who could save a bear, but not a young man in love?"

"You are basing all of this on the assumption that she gave us the remedies with malice in her heart. Maybe they just weren't made to suit humans."

"I know Natalsa, knew her before, and know her anew. She gave me every reason to believe that she was being forthright, she is simply underhanded, as are most of her kind."

"*Her kind?* What do you even recall of her kind prior to the Purging?"

"Need I draw your attention to the demon incident?"

Emmaline bit her lip, and the words that almost came out with them. "Nobody was with her that night, nobody knows the details of what she did. Other than the fact that she opened the rift to send them back from whence they came."

"None of my order have dealings with the Desinders. We have objectives, but –"

"You don't see them have dealings with infernals. But tell me this then, since you are blinded to your follower's behaviors. You remember Natalsa's most infamous encounter, tell me one of the things Leon did prior to the night of the purging? Where did you two first meet?"

"Daughter, not this argument, we settled this last time and I told you then, I refuse to humor your little theories any further."

"They are not theories, and if you would open your glazed and sleep deprived eyes long enough to detect the hour of the day you would see like I do." She stood up, and forgot where she was. She fell backwards into her chair as they went over a bump.

"Emmaline, you are grieving, that is why you are bringing up these things. Please, let's not argue any further. I am weary."

"That much is evident." Emmaline stated and she let her head rest against the cushion behind her.

"Dinner is to be ready when we arrive home. Will you see to it that some is brought to me dear?"

"I'll make sure you're fed."

Long had she suspected Leon of being dangerous, and with every passing day she grew to fear him more. There was so much unsaid behind those sly lips and slick tongue. He never seemed as tired as her father, though he was supposed to be his chief assistant. But more, she wondered who was really assisting whom? It was right there that she decided that she had had enough of getting clouded answers from her father. She was tired of seeing Leon sneaking around the manor and the village as if he was the would-be king. The Forks of Elkshead, and Natalsa, was only a few weeks away by foot. But by horseback, well, it wouldn't take her very long to make a trip there to confront the witch herself.

It wasn't the best plan, and she could have done with some more thinking on it she supposed. But once she was decided on something, her mind was set. As she returned home and saw to it that her father had food, and that the hour was late. Carefully she packed a change of clothes, a cloak, papers proving her identity, and enough fruits. She crept out of her room when the moon rose in the sky, and she heard her father downstairs working. She placed her hands on the door and said a little prayer. "I will go to fix this, Papa. And I hope you forgive me." Blowing him a kiss goodbye, she exited the home and got her horse out of its stable.

She lifted herself into the saddle and secured her pack around her back. "Come on, Precious. We're going away for a while." And the horse began to pick up speed. On and on they traveled through the night. They passed tradesmen camping on roads, so she kept her cloak drawn over her face as much as possible. She did not want to be tracked.

Onwards she rode, until the thriving villages of the central realm faded into fields of barley and corn. And with the passing of those fields, came the fields of desolation, where naught grew but dust. The moon was nearing the end of its journey by the time she breached the top of the hill that overlooked The Forks of Elkshead. It was a well-situated village, with walls that resembled baked mud, yet they appeared sturdier. There was a massive forest that stretched the distance of the village, and small streams flowed close by. The embargo clearly had not occurred yet, for she saw none camping outside to enforce the restriction of trade. There were no fires burning, and no bodies to speak of.

But if the embargo on The Forks was anything like what Leon had led in the past towards people who had rejected Estil's teachings, the village would not last. She stared at the rising smoke that snaked out of chimney tops and wondered which one of them belonged to Natalsa. Somewhere in the village she brewed, and she knew. She would have answers about Leon, about the Remedy, and about her Dagger. All she had to do was find the witch.

She dropped from her horse, and led it by its reigns into the village. She was stopped at the limits by a small collection of farmers. "Hello, miss. Mighty early to be out for a ride, isn't it?" One hailed her.

"It's a mite late for a ride, for mine has just ended you see."

The farmers looked taken aback. "From whence did you come?"

"From the east, and I come to seek your Witch, Natalsa of the Brim by name. Can you tell me where I might be able to find her?"

The farmers looked at each other confusedly. "Why, she left for the woods some hours ago, her house is that way past the blacksmith. You can hitch your horse at our stables which is just past the Lawman's office. Center of town, can't really miss it. You'd do well to wait for her to return, I wouldn't advise one as young and fine looking as you to go into the woods."

"Thank you." She bowed, and led Precious on. She felt something stirring within her, and couldn't tell if it was anxiety or something more benevolent. She prayed for the latter.

✚ Chapter Nine ✚

She was easily recognizable, even without the wide brimmed black hat she had worn back home. Though her features were leaner now, and her eyes dull, she still carried herself the same. Emmaline observed her carefully as she emerged from the forests, and behind her sure as sunrise, was her bear. Standing as tall as she was when just on all fours, with black rippling fur and a peaceful face. It was bizarre to watch them, the unlikeliest of pairs, walk together as allies.

If Natalsa recognized her or not, she wasn't certain, but their eyes locked. Emmaline felt her stomach flutter, as her old savior came closer. Emmaline put one hand behind her back, and bowed at the waist while keeping her eyes locked on Natalsa's. And she spoke words which had not been spoken in years, at least, not to Natalsa.

"Hail, Maiden. May the earth's blessings be upon you, and may your kindness be shown unto me, an outsider."

Natalsa's face screwed up in recognition, and she returned the bow, though slowly. "Peace, daughter, and may you have twice the number of blessings. What kindness can I show thee?" She put her hand on the bear and motioned for her to approach.

"You are very nearly as I remember you, Natalsa. I wonder, do you recognize me?" Emmaline asked, and pulled back her cloak and revealed her entire face.

"Your face is the one who last showed me kindness in Whittle's Bend, it could not be forgotten." She smiled. "I assure you, no thanks is necessary."

Emmaline received her words and confirmed her faith in the witch. "Oh, Natalsa. I told father you hadn't meant for it to happen."

She squinted at her. "Hadn't meant for *what* to happen?"

She licked her chapped lips and ran her hands through her hair nervously. "My Anthony was taken by the Malady, for whatever reason, your methods failed. Father is considering your actions intentional, and is in process of placing an embargo on this village as a result."

She looked to the ground, and turned on her heel. "Come with me. We have much to discuss." She made a clicking sound. "Come, Torga." The bear stretched and followed her. Emmaline kept stride.

"I valued what your father and I decided when we last met. I would have given him the remedy even without his guarantee of my magic being returned. For your sake. The magic was simply the extra sweetness at the bottom of the jar. I am so sorry to hear about your betrothed, I am confident he was a wonderful person."

"Your sympathy is received, and appreciated. Truly, he is still with me, and I feel his loss daily. But I cannot pretend that is my only reason in coming here. For years, memories have tested my grip on sanity, and I must relate them to someone who will listen, and not dismiss them as childhood imaginings."

"I will hear you, and tell you what I believe. Please, do not tarry any longer." Natalsa said, as she directed her into her home. She saw the witch look both ways before shutting the door. They sat at a table, and looked across from each other.

"So much of what I believe all revolves around the night of the purging. And to get to my point quickly, for without your assent in the following, the rest of my ramblings would be wasted breath. Do you remember anything of Leon prior to that night?"

"Of course, Leon was your father's second in command. His guard and confidante. They had known each other since they were boys."

"And then, knowing this response, can you tell me his mother's name? His father's?"

She shook her head. "I do not recall them. I believe they died when he was young."

"Okay, and if I ask you his surname?"

Natalsa hesitated.

"Good." She felt herself grow warm. "What girls in the village fancied him? What did he always bring to the Evenmorn Festivals?"

"My head begins to hurt. What is this? What have you found?"

"Natalsa, it is my firmest conviction that Leon never existed in our village prior to the night of the purging. Do you remember *any* issues the villagers had to your kind? Do you remember any unrest prior?"

"I...I can scarcely recall anything of that kind. He is enlightened, isn't he?" Natalsa asked, and before she could respond, Natalsa got up and snapped her fingers. "He has bewitched the village. Certainly that is what one can assume from this line of thinking!"

"You and I are of one mind." Emmaline clapped her hands joyfully.

"And you remember because of the Dagger." There was no question in her voice.

"That is what I believe, yes. Its imbued magic has kept me out of his spell all these years.

"Well, that blade was blessed by my coven mother. She was talented." She scratched her head. "We have much to think about. Tell me more of your theories."

Emmaline took a deep breath. "I believe my father is the mouthpiece for Leon, and that he is more affected by his magic than any other. I also know that my father is engaged in dark research, early in the mornings I smell the odor of decay and rot emanating from the cellars. I cannot fathom what he does, but it leaves him exhausted and grim. Leon is seen coming and going, playing the act of peon to master, but he avoids me. He believes I am a problem, of this I have no proof, but I have an unnerved feeling when I am around him."

Natalsa gave a sound to her thoughts. "It is possible my cure was not flawed, but that Leon sabotaged it. If he has the magic with him, it could be very possible. Perhaps this entire affair is his plan, pin the death of your beloved on me, starve out my city, and claim the eradication of one more witch."

"Natalsa, you don't know?" Emmaline was in wonder.

"Know what?"

"There are no more witches, Leon keeps a log of everyone he has had killed. You are the only name in his list not marked off, he keeps it framed at the town hall in a place of honor." She grimaced. "I'm sorry. I really am." She looked to Natalsa for a sign of understanding. She felt hot, as if she were being scrutinized.

"Weird and sinister though that is, I should not be surprised. Though I truly am. That is sickening. Your father promised me to restore magic to other witches." She leaned over the table, eyes accusatory.

"It is likely my father is not in his right mind as well, I have tried to break his disillusionment, but he cannot see past the dream he is in."

Natalsa sat down, and held her face in her hands. "Dearest powers."

"I'm sorry, Natalsa. But please, do not give up. We are intelligent, and your village is strong. We can figure out a way to set things right."

"How far does Leon's aspiration travel?" She scoffed. "Have you stopped to think about that? Once I am gone, if I am truly the last, what is to stop him from breaking your father's control just as he broke ours? What all does he desire, and what will he do to get it?"

"We cannot know that. But we cannot wait to find out the answers the hard way." She said pleadingly. She reached out to touch Natalsa's hand, needing to be comforted herself.

"Curse that bastard." Natalsa scowled.

"That's my idea." Emmaline said, feeling braver than she ever had.

Natalsa raised her eyebrow. "Oh?"

"Leon has banished your power, but did he banish the knowledge? Do you not yet still know by heart all the words of power you were taught? Can you not still perform your rites under the moon and have them be heard, yet unable to act?"

Natalsa seemed to light up, and she began to nod. "You wish for me to teach you." She began to smile.

"Make me your weapon in this coming battle. But not just me, make all of us. Anyone who wants to learn from you, break the doctrine and teach men and children. Save the craft before it is corrupted by him." Emmaline hoped she didn't sound like she was pleading too much. She had wanted this for years, and it was so close.

"You are certain about Leon?" She raised her head, looking at her carefully, as if still trying to make up her mind.

"I have no doubt in me."

"And you, with near no understanding of what you ask, are willing to take on the mantle of Witch and subordinate yourself to its teachings?"

"I will subordinate myself to you and *your* teaching." She smiled. "Father didn't have *all* the books in your old home burned. Many of them I have hidden away in my secret places. What I can interpret, I absorb. How else did I know the greeting for witches?"

Natalsa didn't speak for a very long minute. When she did, it was slowly and purposefully. "I have never taken an apprentice. And I do not do so lightly now. It is quite possible the words I would teach you will turn to ash in your mouth, and have no more power than a pinch of pepper under an old man's nose."

"I believe it will work. I believe in what you once were."

"I believe that you believe that. But you will soon learn that if this is successful, and we are able to train a militia of witches, they have the same magic. All the magic is the same, and until you're willing to give everything to it, and receive nothing back but sleepless nights, and an overflowing repertoire of incantations, will it begin to work for you. This is the hardest thing you will have to endure."

"Am I not enduring Anthony's passing with grace? How much harder could this teaching be to endure than knowing that I may never love another again, and I will never feel his lips upon mine?" Her lips trembled, and she tried to control her emotions.

Natalsa got up from the table, and stared right into her eyes. It was unsettling, and she could feel Natalsa's breath on her hot and strong. "You are about to find out."

"I am ready." Emmaline said, and stood to get up.

"Oh no," Natalsa said, putting a hand on her shoulders. "We begin tonight, and understand I am not a teacher, I will push you harder than you have ever been pushed before, and I will not try to stop you from breaking. For such was my instruction when I was young."

"I will do this for my father, and for the rights that have been revoked from your..." she paused "from our kind."

Natalsa smiled at her. "Then let us begin your first lesson, and see if this idea of yours holds water."

Natalsa left Emmaline to practice her memorization exercises, it would take her a little while, but it was how she had learned. Natalsa had been working with her for all of the morning and part of the afternoon. She reckoned that by this time Thomas would be back into town from his errands, and it was to him that she needed to speak most urgently. She left Torga at home dozing in the back yard, and pulled her hair back into a long ponytail. It was hot, and she envied Torga's shady tree.

She walked through the village, taking a moment to smile at each villager as she went, knowing that soon they would be facing hardship due to her. She hoped that she was worth the effort, she would have left already had Thomas not forbidden her. She was nervous about facing Thomas, she still felt guilt over her time with Estil in the tent, and her dreams had lately been plagued by her kissing Thomas instead of Estil. She would deal with that, surely enough.

"Thomas." She hailed him from a distance, and he waved to her, unaware of the doom that was rolling towards them.

"Hey there." Thomas said goodbye to Chubbs, and walked towards her.

"Thomas, I have grave news."

He froze. "Another case of the Malady?" His expression was troubled.

"Though related, it is not why I see you now."

"Well, come then. Sit." He walked over to the bench in the cemetery where that had sat that first day.

"The remedy I gave to Estil failed to cure the boy, he died, and Estil believes that I sabotaged him. He is dropping the agreement and he is leading an embargo against us. I have with his daughter, Emmaline, and there is much more to explain so please do not interrupt me."

He listened intently to what was being said, and there reached a point where he began to smile. Natalsa had to stop him from getting up and calling people over. All the same, they were gaining attention. People were gawking, finding reasons to keep walking past them.   Thomas took out his musket and stared at it. Once Natalsa reached the point about taking Emmaline as her apprentice, and Emmaline's idea about the powers of witchcraft, Thomas nodded gleefully. "I like it."

"Shush." She put a finger on his lips.

"I'm quite excited at all this, it's been so long since I've had a reason to rabble. And Leon sounds like a worthy target. As I mentioned, I do love my form of righteous judgement."

"I worry that I am putting others in danger." She paused and shouted at Penelope who was carrying the same basket of apples over and over, her neck craned over to listen as he passed. "Penny, get home!" Natalsa laughed, despite the current conditions.

"Well, regardless, Leon is the real threat if all of this is to be believed. I think you would find many in the village who are willing to learn under you. Though, there may be those willing to flee and have no part in it."

"I worry little about those who would run, for some of them it should be encouraged. They will not make it easy on us if what my apprentice says is true."

"Can I have an apprentice?" Penny shouted from the gate of the cemetery?"

Natalsa threw a chunk of dirt at her. She dodged it.

"I've gotten faster at dodging things since I lost my eye. It was all fun and games prior to that, but now it has gotten to be serious." Penny shouted as she finally did head home.

"Pain in my spine, that one." Natalsa shook her head gently.

"Natalsa, what world is this when he won't even listen to his own daughter?"

"It is a world where witchcraft is used wrongly, and makes a person do something they would never in their right mind do."

"I suppose is such control is possible, then Estil is innocent as anyone. We should inform everyone just as fast as we can. We must begin to train more men in defensive tactics, and we should stockpile as much water as we can. Who knows how long it will be before magic can offer us any respite."

Natalsa looked at Thomas's hands, and felt an impulse to reach out and hold them. He noticed her staring, and placed his hands upon hers. "It's alright to be afraid. I'm here, and I will make sure you stay safe."

She felt guilty, but held on to his hands at last. "I don't deserve your friendship."

"You cured the Malady, I did not specify that the heal had to apply to humans." He winked.

"I don't mean that, I brought all of this trouble to your door."

"What you did was stop the Seekers from coming to our door and making us as they are."

They got up together, unprompted. "Will you be learning, Thomas?"

"The magic?" He laughed. "I use steel and gunpowder for my magic. It is all the faith I need."

She smiled, and tilted her head. She almost leaned in to touch his lips. He seemed to be waiting, and seeing his willingness, she felt guilt over her time with Estil. She faked a smile instead, and walked away. "I'll see you shortly."

Natalsa returned home and checked on Emmaline's progress. "Apprentice, how goes your exercises?"

"I think I spent at least a good hour perfecting the curl in this letter, but now I am not sure if I even did it right. What do you think?" She thrust a scrap of parchment under Natalsa's nose.

Natalsa took it, and rotated it upside down. Then another ninety degrees. "Which letter is this?"

"The really difficult one to draw."

"It's four strokes." Natalsa said, flabbergasted.

Emmaline's face fell and she buried it in her hands.

"It's alright, you've just started. Inscription is difficult at the start, and I hardly expect you to be doing much of it immediately. We need to test to see if this magic is even possible for you. We are going to test you on the most basic of spells. And you will need to let me know if you feel anything funny happen."

"What must I do?"

"You are going to be casting a warding spell, it is a simple form of protection, used on rings and bracelets. Your wristband will work fine. Imagine yourself in a small, cramped room. You aren't even able to extend your arms out from your body. Picture a small white star at the core of your being, imagine it glowing brighter and brighter as you hold on to your bracelet. And keep going until the light has completely taken up the space of your mind, and it is all you see in your vision of yourself. When that has happened, Thank the spirit of light for being a good power, and ask them for the blessing of protection on your bracelet. After that is done, hold your tongue until you feel something happen. I will let you know if we need to stop."

"What will I feel?" She closed her eyes.

"I can't answer it for you, for me, it is a tingle on my tongue and a rush of chills on my skin. Other times, it is just fire in my chest."

"Fire? Does it hurt?" She asked naively.

"It cleanses all evils away, and leaves only refined energy. You are better for it. Fear nothing that comes from magic if your intentions are pure." Natalsa could hear her excitement in her own tone, and realized how greatly she hoped this to work.

"What would happen if your intentions are not pure?"

"Eventually, it would catch up to you. Evil turns on itself, it always does. But how long must the innocent suffer until justice is measured?"

"Okay, let's start I suppose, teacher." She sounded uncertain of herself.

Natalsa walked over and wrapped her arms around Emmaline's shoulders. "Do not lose faith now, after it has driven you so far." She said comfortingly, and surprisingly felt better herself.

Natalsa watched her apprentice, and she was patient. She waited and counted the seconds in her mind, visualizing a ring swaying back and forth on a string above her palm. She listened to her breathing, and Emmaline's. She lit a stick of incense in hopes that it would further ease her nerves. Natalsa was just putting out the flame when she saw a shimmer of light from behind her. She turned, mouth agape, and saw the star glowing at the core of her apprentice, whose eyes were still closed, but her mouth was smiling joyously. "Natalsa, I feel something."

"By all the stars..." Natalsa swore, and took a seat before she fell. "I should say you do."

From outside the village, a convoy of Seekers on horseback came to a halt. There were only forty of them so far, but there would be more. The head of the company was Calvin, and he wore a red sash around his robes, and a smile was stretched across his sunburned face. He would not be saddened this day, as he dreamed of what would come. They had taken longer to get here than they had anticipated, but they had to stop at neighboring villages.

At each village they stopped and spread the story of what had occurred to Anthony at Natalsa's hands. They stirred up the people, as they had been stirred the night of the purge, and many swore to follow them to haze The Forks of Elkshead. Already, Calvin had seen traders turn from the Forks roads and head back towards more settled regions of the land.

He instructed his men to construct the command tent, which was naturally large and luxurious. Fire pits were dug, and tie-outs for the horses were hastily constructed along with armory chests. The light of the sun fell from the sky as evening wore on, and they became comfortably inebriated. The first night of an embargo was typically the most fun for Calvin. This was his fifth campaign, and the last town they had hazed, Odom's Haven, had fallen within a week. The women were loose enough to save their own lives; some of the boys had been as well. For this village, Calvin had only one conquest in mind.

"Balthus, I want you to prepare our casters. Once the night has fallen I want the sky to light up with our flames. And our Messenger." He grinned.

"It is already ready, Calvin."

"This is why I like you, Brother Balthus. You think."

"I try to make a habit of it."

As the stars began to light the sky, another source of light filled the air. A radiant seraph was seen hovering over The Forks of Elkshead, and all the people in The Forks wondered about it.

"To the inhabitants of the Forks of Elkshead, I am the Messenger of Estil the Seeker. On this night, we shall visit your homes and claim no less than five lives. It is in your best interest to flee this city at once, for any remaining by the morning will be given no quarter, all lives will be forfeit. You hold among you a witch who has committed crimes against the Seekers. Justice will be had. Already, we have cut off your supplies, and your neighbors revile you. For they have heard of your habits. You will surrender the witch, in the end, or this entire village will be burned."

The seraph vanished from the sky, but for those who had stared at it, the image still burned in the back of their eyelids and their minds still heard the echoing promises of destruction that was their inheritance. People discussed hurriedly among themselves on what they ought to do, and Thomas cursed the harriers, for he had not expected them to come so fast. He hadn't gotten to inform the town, and now there would be panic.

"It didn't have to be this way. We could have done this honorably." He said, staring out the window and grabbing hold of his sword and musket. "You will rue the day, Leon. I swear on my life."

And the night descended again upon the town, and Natalsa stood defiantly alongside Emmaline, trusting in her apprentice.

+ BOOK TWO +

+ CHAPTER ONE +

NOBODY SLEPT THE NIGHT of the Seraph, all through the hours of the night the people were in a tizzy trying to determine the best path for themselves. It was determined by many that they would stay, and that surprised Natalsa more than a little. She hadn't slept herself, and instead worked with Emmaline on her spell craft.

As the morning sun broke at the horizon she waited, uncertain of what indication she would receive that something went wrong. But the morning came, and the sun rose, and there were none dead. Nothing at all appeared wrong, and it was unsettling. She had expected some form of death, danger, or calamity. She walked to Chubb's pastry stand and saw him sprinkling powdery sugar onto some hot rolls. "Good morning, you seem to be the lady of the hour."

"Oh, don't we all know it now." She took out a coin and laid it upon his stand and picked up a cherry pastry. "I feel like something should have happened by now."

"Should we complain to someone?" Chubbs asked, fighting a grin. "Personally I'm quite grateful."

"I'm not saying I'm not. I'm just saying if they are hesitating, one wonders why." She tilted her head and bid her friend farewell.

"Stay safe, dear." He waved goodbye to her. "And in case you ever wondered, you're my favorite witch." He chuckled.

She laughed with him a moment. "I'll be careful." She gave him a quick hug, not certain if it was a welcome move. But his strong arms wrapped around her, and he smelled of baked goods. It was nice, and she was sad when it ended. "In case you ever wondered, you're my favorite baker."

"I'm the only baker." He shrugged.

"And I'm the only witch." She grinned.

"It doesn't mean any less to me." Chubbs smiled, and waved her off.

Natalsa prowled around in the early morning, and listened to the stir of people wakening, those fortunate souls who had found sleep. Natalsa made her way to the front of the gates of the village, and stared out at the expanse between her village and the Seekers. She strained her eyes to make out details, they were quite far away. There were surely no more than forty men, but if they were all magic users, that was more than she alone could hope to overcome.

She was turning to leave when she felt the fire in her calves rise to her lower back and scale up to her chest. She started to speak but instead wished for air that seemed slow in coming. She put her hands out to steady herself as she stumbled, but fining nothing, she fell face first into the cobblestone.

"What in the name of all that is good is this?" She clutched at her chest. "This is terrible!" She moaned loudly. She saw stars, and felt as if all the wind had been expunged from her lungs. She clutched at her head and felt a lump forming, squishy and protruding from her forehead. She rose clumsily to her feet and turned around to see a glowing light around some figures in the distance, she understood the magic had come from them, and she teared up. They laughed, she could hear it carrying over the distance. "If I had but an iota of my power, our positions would be reversed." She struggled to move out of sight, and on impulse, began knocking on doors.

"Get up. Get up and get to town hall." She knocked on windows, banged on doors, and clapped her hands. People poked their heads out of their homes and looked at her as though she was mad. "You each have a choice to make this morning. The Seeker's threat fell flat, but they are starting spell work to anyone in range. Get up!"

She was overtaken by a fit of coughing so severe that several people came out to care for her. "What can we do Natalsa? Can I bring you anything?" She heard someone ask, but her fit was so intense she could barely breathe. Tears streamed down her face. "Get to town hall." She managed to squeak out. She turned her thoughts inward and was terrified that this was just the beginning of a serious curse.

She unsteadily made it to her feet, and hobbled along as quickly as she could. But she kept throwing glances over her shoulders, up to the skies, certain that she was being watched. She got better the further she went, but the fear was there now.

Bursting into Thomas home, Natalsa roused him from sleep and yelled at him to get ready.

"What gives you the right to barge in here so early, Natalsa? I hadn't been asleep for more than an hour!" He groaned, sounding pathetic.

"Cry to your mother." She said, slamming the door behind her.

The village gathered, those young and old, and into the town hall they went. Natalsa ordered two soldiers to stand watch at the gates to make sure the Seekers didn't try anything. "Sound the alarm at once if you see them move one bit. They are pain personified. I can speak from experience."

Natalsa moved down the center aisle and saw the townsfolk looking at her, even Thomas gave her room to speak. She felt her robes flow around her, and she had always liked the way it felt. She thought it made her seem more important. Today it seemed she was.

"Friends, you have known me and what I am for a long time now. I will tell you plainly, we are under embargo as some of you may have already heard, and it is due to the ruler of the Seekers being under a spell by an evil man. It is my belief that should we simply incapacitate the man I know as Leon, then order can be restored along with Estil's sanity. With him in the right frame of mind, we may be able to end any violence before this gets out of hand." She motioned everyone to draw in closer, as she heard questions coming from the crowd.

"They've told us the reason we're under embargo is because you gave a faulty cure." Caroline stated, as she held her daughter Marawny to her side.

"I gave the man the same remedy as I did Torga, I cannot explain why it failed." She clasped her hands together pleadingly.

"They have also told us you have kidnapped his daughter." Furler, the academic, spoke. "Is that who has been in your home these days?" He pointed at Emmaline, who was near the front of the gathering.

"Furler, I have taken an apprentice, and it is Estil's daughter. She is the one who informed me that her father is outside his mind, and has likely been so since I myself was driven from my home. Be patient, and I will tell you all that I know."

"Will you not tell us your side, and not theirs?" He curled his beard with his fingers, and stared at her.

"It has been revealed to me, that I am the last of the Witches, and Leon has eradicated all others. It does not matter if this is true information, or false to me. The possibility that it could be is all that matters." She paused to look Furler in the eyes. She saw him nod at her, as if he understood. She had to presume it meant he did.

"Family, If I fall, and Leon is truly in charge of the Seekers, imagine the world and what it could become. This is a man who committed genocide against my people in the dead of night as we slept. We had children, we had husbands, and all of them were slaughtered." She snapped her fingers. "They were dead without a trial. Their deaths prolonged as the flames consumed their flesh." She walked around animatedly. She took out flint, and set flame to a candle in her robes. "Do you want to feel what the flames taste like? They are unforgiving. And we were made to die to them." She felt tears starting, and willed herself to control her emotions.

"This is, and there are no maybes, this is the only chance we will have to fight against him before he realizes his dreams. You have seen the good I have done here for your families, and though I cannot yet determine the reason the remedy fails on humans, I am closer than any other has been. Closer than Marie, closer than Ixtarae. Closer than Elina. You can take chances with me, or you can take chances that Leon will treat all of you fairly once I am ashes. But look at what he has done already." She looked at as many of the town as she could. She saw Thomas. She saw Chubbs. She saw Guy. She watched the babies cradled in their mother's arms. The tears fell freely at this point, and she gave in to her sadness.

"I prefer living. And I believe in you." Guy said, as he put his arm around Penelope. Her friend stared at her with her other eye patched, and couldn't smile any wider.

"We are both with you." Penelope said. "And to Hell with the Seekers and their corruption! Let's smack some foulness right out of them!"

"What is it you propose we do?" Furler said, looking directly at her with his hands open wide.

"I have taken my first apprentice, and it has been shown to me through her that my magic is not dead, whatever evil Leon committed only applied to the witches of the world at that time. I will give you my words, and my knowledge, and to whomever is willing to take a stand, I will teach you. In the old times, it was restricted to those we found worthy, and never to men or children." She stared up at the skies, and hoped that they would not strike her down with lightning.

"But in this world, the world that is on the brink of collapse, we cannot be so prudish. Trust in me, and I will let you know the experience of flames coursing through your blood, you will feel the rush of cooling absoluteness all around you, and you will affect change. You will experience the pure ecstasy of my people. Only together will we be able to lead this front, I need all of you. Who will stand with me?" Natalsa plead with them, kneeling and holding her arms out towards them in an open embrace. "Will you? Will you please?" She pulled her hair back, and tried to make eye contact with everyone gathered. The baker. The spinster. The teachers. The drunkards. "You are all my people, and I will protect you. But I need your help to do so. Give me the chance."

"What if we die?" Gretchen the spinster woman asked.

"No, what if we live?" Lemuel offered, grinning. "I could have a drink to that victory."

"I don't want to die." Gretchen said as she got up and left the town hall. "I'm leaving. Now." She got up and some folk began to follow her. Benches began to scrape the floor, and Natalsa felt her hope flounder. "Please listen to me, hear me!" Natalsa cried, and Emmaline came to stand next to her, consolingly.

"I am too old to learn anything new; can't we help in other ways?" Millicent asked. "I can treat wounds."

"We will not turn away any help, but imagine the wounds you could cure with magic! Wonderful restoration as you've never known!" Natalsa's face grew hot with the light of the morning sun. She wiped the sweat from her brow and stood up. "We can work wonders together."

"I have my babies to consider. Will they grow up without a mother?" Judith the teacher spoke up.

"I have grown without a mother, and thanks to what is happening I might be growing older without a father." Emmaline spoke passionately. "Death claims us all. It is how we live that matters. Would you have your children knowing you were a coward?" Emmaline stared at Judith.

"I would have –" Judith began.

"Natalsa." Furler interrupted loudly.

She looked to him, and saw his grim face brighten. "I am not too old, and I am always willing to know more. Perhaps there is more learning to be had in the real world, than a schoolhouse." Furler said, and he got up, and embraced the witch.

Judith stared at him wide-eyed, and quite embarrassed looking. "Well I never meant that I wouldn't join you. I just had questions!" Judith said, as she quickly followed Furler.

He was the catalyst that was needed, for soon others were getting up, and they crowded the witch, placing their arms around whoever was closest. Natalsa felt their acceptance, and held their trust in her hands. It was a delicate and precious feeling, and she did not hold back the tears that streamed down her cheeks. "I will not fail any of you. We begin immediately, meet me in my backyard, and bring food. I haven't hardly enough for everyone, but within a good week or two, that may change if we can manage the spell correctly."

In Natalsa's back yard many of the villagers huddled, some even daring to pet Torga for the first time. Thomas was there, standing stoically at Natalsa's side along with Emmaline. "Is this her then? The girl?" Furler asked curiously.

"I am Emmaline, daughter of Estil and the first initiate of Natalsa. I am glad to see you are here. I believe you will find all this life changing. Already, I feel the stir of the universe in my body."

"Well that sounds incredibly impressive." Furler said as he bit into an apple.

The townspeople all looked to Natalsa, and she looked back at each of their faces. She had a small militia all at her disposal. She saw the faces of the elderly, the middle aged, and most inspiring of all were the faces of the children. They held their parent's hands, some of them barely entering their teenage years. She looked at men, who would be the first indoctrinated by the Witches Craft as it was taught to Natalsa. It was unreal, knowing that when she had awoken yesterday morning she had been just herself, but now here today she was teacher to all of them.

"We are going to get started by the most basic of magics, once we have mastered it, and it should not take long, we will be moving on to offensive magics. If you can all start by speaking clearly . . ." Natalsa instructed her militia, and the attention on the people was hers.

+ CHAPTER TWO +

THE SEEKERS GREW IN number daily, and Natalsa observed them from atop the rafters of a home near the border of the town. She hadn't seen a trade caravan in over a week. And sometimes she would see people ride up to the Seeker's on horseback, they did not look like magic users, indeed some of them had children alongside. They would point, make gestures and then leave. She was beginning to think that her village was being made spectacle of, and people were coming to see for themselves. Natalsa was observing just such a group this morning when they did something that no others had done.

They came closer.

They were holding bright objects in their hands, and they were running gaily in her direction. She tried to make out if there was a threat, and suddenly realized what was happening. They were throwing fruit, rotten vegetables, and mud. They chucked them at and over the walls, to come soaring down on anyone unfortunate enough to be close. Natalsa was such a person this morning. The cucumber and mud pelted her and clung to her hair, causing her to hurl profanities at them. "Witch! Witch! Burn the witch!" They cried as they continued to throw vileness.

"Murderer of the young! May your womb wither and be barren as the desert!" The outsiders called, and cackled as they shook their fists at her. "Murder anyone else recently, devil woman?"

She set her jaw firm and shook the debris from her as well as she could, and left her observation platform. "I don't need this today. The fools." She prayed for them against every intention she had to do otherwise.

But that was hardly the worst of it. The Seekers encouraged travelers to take their relief in one of a series of chamber pots, and then they would let the travelers toss the contents at the Forks walls. Natalsa climbed up to her outpost every morning and watched this happen, and she marveled at perfect strangers who demonstrated such fear and hatred. She grew weary, each day was harder. She was not sure what the Seekers were waiting on.

"Perhaps they're trying to see how far the insults will go." Thomas offered. As a shout sounded at that exact moment. "Your mother would have been better to choke you off at the start." She had tried to not cry after that one, but she loved her mother, her mother had been the kindest person she knew. She could only imagine the enjoyment the Seekers were getting from this. The only enjoyment Natalsa felt was when she decided that she couldn't take their words personally, and she forgave them for their ignorance.

With each successive insult, each direct hazing of her town, she became more resolved towards training her apprentices, and having something to fight with before the Seeker's got bored of hazing, and went to full out assault.

The sun was just peeking out over the forest, and she had just finished climbing up to her lookout. She held a cup of tea in one hand and sipped it softly. She realized something was amiss, and after scanning the usual spot at which the Seeker's usually rallied, she discovered what was wrong. The seekers themselves had moved closer to the village, and she saw them looking up at her, smiling deviously.

Calvin's voice sounded loudly and broke the silence of the morning. "To the witch protectors in the Forks of Elkshead, we have made our demands clear to you. Yet you have defied us these weeks. You have lost all access to trade, gained the hatred of all neighboring villages, and still have more to lose! Surrender Natalsa unto us, and you shall be pardoned. You have the span of one hour, at which time we will begin our assault."

Natalsa made a sound of disbelief, finished her tea, and walked to town square. It was no surprise to her to see her apprentices awake and ready. There were but seven of them who had made it past the hurdles of the first rites; Emmaline, Penelope, Guy, Furler, Chubbs, Mari, and Simon. And of course, their personal *outsider,* Thomas. Natalsa smiled at him, and he returned the gesture. Things had been good the last three weeks, despite the embargo, and she found herself missing magic less and less the more she missed him.

"I'm sure you have all heard that man." She said, looking to each of them. "That man is Calvin, and he is the reason Penelope is blind in one eye. He is cruelness, and the very wickedness that he thrusts upon me. You have heard him, he will not reason. He will simply do whatever he wants, regardless of consequence. You must be prepared for him."

"You're all a bunch of fools, fighting against the Seekers."

Natalsa turned to see Gretchen with bags in tow. "I wouldn't leave were I you, Gretchen."

"To the devil with your advice, witch. I'm getting out of here before we all starve." Gretchen huffed and waddled along with bags under her arms.

"Wasn't she supposed to leave already?" Simon asked, standing on his tip toes to get a look at her. His small frame struggled to stay balanced, and he nearly fell.

"Yes, and she has made her choice long ago." Emmaline advised him, catching the young boy before he did bodily harm.

"Disregard her. We must focus on keeping those here safe. I am uncertain how the Seekers will attack, but I know we should be able to repel some of what they perform. The advantage is with us, they think they will face simple villagers. They do not know about any of you, nor how many of you there are. Today will be ours."

The hour passed, and Natalsa walked boldly to the front of the town, Thomas was at her side. She shouted as clearly as she could, and her throat hurt, they were so accustomed to speaking silently. "To the Seekers, I am Natalsa, and I do not have intentions of surrendering myself, or this town, to your whims. I give you this opportunity to leave, and to send my regards to your leaders."

She looked at Calvin, who stared back smiling. "I'd hoped that you would say that." He reached into his robes and sprinkled something in a semi-circle around him, and she saw his lips dance. She stood faithfully beside Thomas, and waited. Calvin's hands began to glow orange, and soon a ball of fire erupted towards her. It was almost to her now, and she didn't bat an eyelid. She held up her hand, and spoke clearly "Stop." The fireball fizzled out of sight, she and Thomas were unharmed.

"It appears as though I have more magic than you had been told, Calvin. Perhaps you'd wish to reconsider your aggression before you force me to go on the offensive." Natalsa challenged him, casting a wink to Emmaline who smiled back at her proudly.

Calvin looked perplexed, and looked at his men briefly. "You can deflect a single spell, but we easily outnumber you, and you will eventually tire. Surrender yourself, or your village is forfeit."

"Will that be your position then, Calvin?" Natalsa queried him, and waited for his response.

His response came in the form of raining fire. From the Heavens waves of fire came rushing towards the village and Natalsa continued her part of the act. She dramatically extended both arms to their furthest reaches and shouted "Mother Earth, bless your servant!" she whipped her head back for effect. From around her she saw her apprentices all moving in unison, the true casters of the spell.

A glowing, wide globe surrounded the Forks, and the fire hit the golden walls and sizzled into nothingness. Natalsa knew that such a feat, for a single witch, would be remarkable. She had never known of a single witch to make it happen, and if they were educated at all, they would be cowed by such a demonstration.

Once the rain of fire ended, Natalsa made a churning motion with her hands and began to whisper her own incantation. Heavy storm clouds rolled in and directly above the Seekers a black rain cloud emptied itself upon them, drenching them alone to the bone. "It is hot enough these Summer days, Calvin. You should cool yourself off." Natalsa shouted at him, smiling deviously.

"You were supposed to be powerless!"

"You will find that I am favored among by the powers. Some might call me *exquisite*. You would do well to not test my true magic. Be gone from here, and pray you do not get ordered to return." Natalsa waved them off, and she saw Calvin consider her. She was certain he wasn't going to turn tail.

Natalsa caught movement out of the corner of her eye, and saw Gretchen fleeing the town quite rapidly now. "I am not part of this! I am simply an old woman trying to flee the devil's kitchen!" She dragged her bags behind her, and rushed towards Calvin's men.

Natalsa saw it happen before she could give any signal, before anyone could anticipate.

Calvin whispered quickly, and his palm glowed vibrant yellow. He slashed upwards and drove his palm into Gretchen's chest, and the smell of burning flesh filled the air. "Her blood is on you, Forks of Elkshead, but most of all you Natalsa." He cackled madly.

Natalsa screamed in rage. "No, devil. Her blood runs down your arm, and I will see the day when that blood is accounted for."

Natalsa wished for the magic now, more than ever. Gretchen might not have agreed with her, but she felt the loss.

"You monster! She was an old woman!" Someone yelled from behind Natalsa. "Innocent as a baby, and look what you did? Do you see what these people are? All of you who are not with them, do you see this? Do you understand?" Natalsa turned and saw Judith weeping, collapsed on her knees.

Calvin laughed and his men laughed with him, though some seemed sickened. "Shall we kill you also?" Calvin shouted, and Judith screeched as she ran back into the safety of the town.

Calvin gave a huge grunt of effort and chucked Gretchen off his hand and toward the city walls. Natalsa heard a thud, and closed her eyes. "You will hear from us shortly. Count your victory." Calvin ordered his men to retreat. Thomas gripped her hand tightly, and took her away from the city gates.

"That was nearly very good." He said, pride still apparent in his voice, though they had suffered a loss.

"Thomas, that was a charade, one that is only good until they realize they are not dealing with me, but 7 initiates." Natalsa said furiously, walking quickly back into the town. The crowds parting for her respectfully.

She heard them offer condolences, that they understood, that she couldn't be blamed.

"Seven initiates being taught by the Brim." Furler said, twirling his chestnut brown mustache and casting her a sly grin. "That was, all things considered I mean, the most fun I've had since I learned to read Pomeran. When do we get to do it again?"

Thomas spent the night with her for the first time that evening. He'd been hesitant to leave at dinner, and after sitting on the bed to continue their dinner conversation, they'd decided not to get up. "I never meant for this to happen." Natalsa said, holding the back of his head with her palm.

"This isn't a bad thing, this is something normal humans do." Thomas whispered at the base of her neck as he kissed her collarbone.

"I don't want to hurt you. I don't want to hurt myself." She tried to stop him, tried to pull him back.

"Then stop doing something you'll regret later." He reached down to her waist, and he breathed heavily.

"Come on now." She said, feeling herself slip into his arms. "I understand tension and releasing, but –"

He silenced her with his affection.

She awoke early, and found him lying beside her, sheets wrapped around half of him. The other half, she admired in the light of the morning which was ripe with reflection. He breathed easily, and she saw long scars along his waist, and upper chest. She wondered about them, and how they came to be there. They did not detract from his appearance, if anything she found herself more trapped by him. She stared up at the ceiling and thought about how she had let Estil have her in the tent during their negotiation. She wasn't involved with Thomas at the time, and had no obligation to anyone. Though she chalked the entire affair up to the heat of the moment, and long periods in between encounters with any man, she still felt guilty.

Estil was the man who had ordered the killings, but then again, he wasn't the man who had ordered the killings. That was on

Leon. This line of thinking made her head pound, and she clenched her fist above her heart. But who had she slept with, was it truly Estil, or was it the Estil under Leon's control? Was the whole affair setup to make her fall and further confuse her? She twisted a finger in her hair, and rolled over to get out of bed. She would simply tell Thomas what had happened, and that would be the end of it. There would be no secrets, and they could have a fresh and promising relationship.

She prepared herself breakfast, and a cup of tea. She took out her journals of the remedies, and began her morning ritual of dissecting what had led her to cure Torga, and what might have gone wrong with Anthony. She did this out of duty to Thomas, but also out of affection for Emmaline, whom she now considered more of a sister than apprentice. "But isn't that the very purpose of witchcraft?" She wondered aloud. The girl was clever, and continuously studying the craft. She thought that perhaps, if she mirrored more of her apprentice, that she might have found the remedy long ago.

Natalsa reread the differences in the original ten concoctions, and spoke them aloud. "Callys Hood, followed by Harbor Ivy, Lemonshade Grass, and basic Munsblade. Reagents past these primers include in order Brinefoam, Fools Bounty, Elder Breath, Dimmer Vine, Sailor's Folly, and Worts Cap."

For days she had ground up the reagents into fine powder and made every possible combination of them as she had during the first trials. All she needed was a patient on which to try them, and this time with tedious documentation, she would know what she did different.

Secretly, she held a fear that something was missing, something so simplistically fundamental that she would kick herself. She wished for an opportunity to test it, horrible though that was to wish on any human being, but no case presented itself. All the same, she continued to experiment.

There was a loud knock on Natalsa's door, and she jumped, having not had very good luck with knocking lately. "Natalsa, it is Piotr, may I please come in?"

The mortician, lovely. She opened the door and invited him into her living room. "Good morning, why do you call so early?" She asked, offering him tea.

"I've been on the search for Thomas, people have said you were the last seen with him. I don't mean to be forward, but is he here? We have a body that needs processing."

Natalsa put down her tea. "A body? Whose?" She clutched his arm desperately.

"It is Gretchen's, Natalsa. The wound was terrible to behold." His bushy eyebrows frowned and made his chocolate eyes seem deeper than usual.

Natalsa frowned, knowing how bad that had sounded. "Of course. I'm sorry, I just thought you meant someone else had died." She patted him. "I'll get him." She said kindly.

"Thank you." His hands were shaking, and she had to wonder how terrible it was to have shaken a mortician this badly.

"Thomas." She said, patting him on his shoulder. He grunted, and stirred slowly. "Thomas, Piotr is here, Gretchen was killed. He needs your signoff for processing."

He sat up, and steadied himself by placing both his arms at their furthest extremities. He shook his head, and looked at her. "Sorry, a bit rough this morning." He coughed into the crook of his arm. "What happened now?"

"It's Gretchen. Piotr is here to process her, but needs your signoff." She said dismally.

"Mm. I should get dressed. You haven't any idea where you threw my pants, do you?" He stifled a yawn.

She tossed him his slacks, and peeked only briefly as he dressed. "Don't be long. We have things to consider today." She reminded him with a pointed finger.

"Of course." He kissed her, and left her home with Piotr in tow.

She heard him cough again before he left, and hoped that he wasn't coming down with anything.

+ CHAPTER THREE +

ESTIL SAW THE LIGHT filtering through moth eaten curtains in his laboratory, and he smelled his stench mixed with the reek of decomposition. He was surrounded by decaying animal corpses, each one desiccated by his experiments, and thrown aside when their usefulness had expired. He heard a knock on the door from above, and gave a shuddering sigh. "Declare yourself." He was unfamiliar with the sound of his own voice, and he realized it startled him, so thin it sounded.

"It is Leon, Estil. Might I come in? I have news that requires your attention."

"Can you not handle it, you useless imbecile." Estil picked up a blackened phial and inspected its contents carefully. He began to pick up a spool of golden thread and carefully wrap the bottle with it.

"It concerns..." Leon began.

"Unless it concerns the location of my daughter I do not want to hear anything of it."

Estil heard nothing for the longest time, and he was about to recite an incantation, when he heard Leon clear his throat.

"She has regained her powers, though we know not how. Our troops just returned stating she could fend off the full might of their assault. It appears as though she is more powerful than she once was."

Estil sat the phial down calmly in its holder, and looked up towards the door at the top of the staircase. "Get down here."

Light poured in from upstairs, and Estil saw Leon descend the stairs, and watched as his lip curled in revulsion. "If the smell bothers you send a maiden, at least then I will expect womanly delicacies."

Leon's lip twitched briefly, but as soon as it was observed, it ceased. "I apologize."

"There is no way she could have regained her powers, Else she would have used them on me and ended my life in the tent."

"Ah, but my lord, did you not have unnatural relations with her that day? Were you perhaps, not under her spell even then?" Leon suggested helpfully.

Estil stared at Leon, and considered it. "I felt an unnatural attraction to the woman, there is no denying it. But for what purpose would she enchant me?"

"Can you think of no reason?" Leon huffed. "There is no greater ransom than the life of a ruler's unborn heir. She was likely prime for breeding and saw her opportunity. Why use magic when extortion is so much more delicious when exacting vengeance?" He chuckled. "Is that not so?"

"You have done much thought on this, Leon." He said accusingly.

"It is my duty to think as such Estil, is it not why you let my heart continue to beat?" He sounded offended, and put a hand over his heart.

Estil grimaced. "If it is true, I cannot allow her to be killed until the child is born. I will not have them murdered because of her insidiousness."

"Should we continue the embargo, lest she starve?" Leon shrugged. "We wouldn't want to harm the baby, if she is with child."

"Perhaps I will speak with her myself, see if I can't use some of my magic on her this time."

"You must know she would never take the risk again." Leon whispered shrilly, and then he looked around him. "By the powers, are you any closer to your goal? How much longer must we endure these cadavers?" He held his nose, and his face turned pale.

"I am nearly ready. I have brought several specimens back to life, and exerted a level of control over them. I am ready for human testing. See to it that one of our men has poison in his meal tonight. Then, see to it that he finds his way here soon thereafter. I trust you will be able to handle his disappearance."

"It will be a non-issue. He will be here before he grows cold." Leon spoke as if this was the most boring thing in the world.

"Is there anything else you need of me? I need to return to work." Estil said huffing loudly.

Leon smiled. "No, Estil. May your work be profitable this evening."

"It will not be long, and we will have the power of life after death." He eyed his advisor. "And with it, an army."

Leon bowed, and took his leave, climbing the stairs quickly. Estil cleared his throat and took a swig of water. He picked up the black vial again and wrapped it in gold twine, softly he pleaded with the powers. "Lords of the Earth, and the realms beyond, hear your servant. Enhance this potion with the essence of undeath, so that even the strings of life may be again whole."

He poured the liquid onto a fox, dead two days, and watched as its whiskers began to twitch. "Frolic, creature, as I command." And the reanimated corpse rose, stared at Estil, and began to race around the room. Estil laughed, and clapped his hands. "Soon."

Emmaline sat cross legged upon the stone wall that surrounded the cemetery and practiced her fire crafting spells. She could conjure the tiniest elemental flame, and it danced around in her palm. She still had burn marks on her right hand, and frost burn marks on her left hand from all the practicing she had done. She focused intently on the torch across the street and willed the elemental to jump over to it, which it did after the briefest delay.

"This is such fun." She laughed, and snapped her fingers, causing the elemental to puff out of existence until he was needed again. She watched the villagers walk hither and yon about their day, shoulders swinging easily with their light steps now that the Seeker's weren't raining fire on them.

It had been over a week since the Seeker's had left. Gretchen's body had been laid to rest. Though she barely knew the woman, she felt pity for her. She only wanted to stay alive. She had long since quit caring about the fate of any seeker, and sought only the redemption of her father. Emmaline was convinced if she could only become powerful enough, she could cease Leon's magic herself and prove to her father that she was right all along. Not that being right mattered, but it certainly validated her intuition.

She saw some young boys playing roughly with a younger girl, pushing her around and teasing her. Emmaline started to get up, but was struck with an idea so clever, she surprised herself. "Rulers of the Earth, hear your daughter, and grant me the power to balance the scales." She took out a rose petal from her inner red robe and placed it on her tongue, chewing it slowly. The tingles running down her arm to her finger tips as she felt the magic.

Next one of the boys tried to push her into a mud puddle, he was pushed back with such power that he ended up falling flat on his rear end, causing all his friends to laugh at him instead. The girl's hands flew to her mouth, and she fumbled to help him up, shouting apologies as she did so. "I'm sorry Lee, I'm so sorry! Here let me help you up!"

Emmaline stifled her laughter, and watched as he accepted the young one's help. The girl was busy talking, but Emmaline could not make out what was being said, instead she watched the other boys admire her from afar. "Well, I doubt she'll be picked on again anytime soon." She smiled, and felt herself grow warm. "Thank you, Rulers. You know just the trick."

"Emma," a voice called from down the street.

She turned to look, and saw Guy waving to her. "Morning, Guy." She hopped from the wall and closed the distance between them. "How goes it?"

"Oh, not well, I'm afraid. Have you seen Thomas? I was wanting to borrow one of his books, but he's not at the town hall. I was hoping you or Natalsa might have seen him."

"Mm, I'm afraid I haven't, and Natalsa has been in the woods since morning. I'll be happy to help you look for him. Did you go to his home?"

"No, I rarely see him there at all, he's so busy." He said staring at his boots.

"Well, I've been up since before the sun rose, and I've not seen him come this way. Let's go check." She said cheerily, as she was in quite a good mood despite the gloom.

"So how is the recording going? I bet you have had more news this last month than the whole history of the Forks." Emmaline said, kicking a rock as she went.

"I'm up to three rolls of parchment, so yes, you could say it's a light read by this point. Though I am happy to be documenting this ugly affair, I do hope it ends soon. I don't think Penny likes the late hours for more reasons than just the burning oil."

"Oh, can't blame her there, handsome." Emmaline teased him.

"Yeah, yeah." Guy said, as he knocked on Thomas's front door.

He knocked again after a few moments. "No, it doesn't seem he is here either."

They were just about to leave when they heard something thud against the door heavily. Emmaline turned, and paused, intently listening. Hearing nothing, she very nearly gave it up as her imagination. But a subtle tug on her heart made her act. She pushed against the door and after a moments resistance it gave way. A smell of vomit reached her, and it nearly sent her backwards in need of fresh air. "Dear lord." She covered her nose with her sleeves and stepped inside urgently.

"Thomas, Thomas are you in here?" She called, with Guy close behind, stepping on her heels.

She heard a groaning from the other room, and continued to walk deeper inside. She had never stepped foot inside Thomas' home, and stepped over an overturned chair and a spilled plate of food. There was a groaning coming from beyond this room, and she kept walking until she entered his bedroom. There was light shining on him, and for a moment, she thought it was just unusual lighting.

And that was when dread, smoldering and fetid washed over her. "Damn it."

Guy leaned over her shoulder and gawked. "Thomas." He choked out, potentially gagging on the air or from shock.

She grabbed Guy's arm. "Go to the forest, find her. Listen for Torga, you'll find her then."

Guy did as he was instructed, and he ungracefully exited the home, knocking over more things as he went.

Emmaline ran into the kitchen, and grabbed a cloth and dipped it in water. She returned to him and placed it on his forehead, which was hot to the touch. "It's alright, Thomas. Natalsa will be here soon."

Thomas groaned, and his bloodshot eyes locked onto hers, and it was there that Emmaline first saw a grown man cry.

Natalsa felt nothing as she laid at Thomas' side, surrounded by empty phials that seemed to do nothing to ease his suffering, or reduce the green tint that was spreading over his body by the hour. Emmaline regularly brought him cool cloths for his head, and Natalsa would dab water onto his lips. She held him, and spoke to him about the first time they had met. She hoped it was helping, for he would or could not speak clearly.

When he fell into periods of rest, she would get up and watch over him. She counted every time his chest rose and fell, and whenever it had seemed too long between breaths she would have to touch him. Maddening fear would grip her until she would feel his breath on her hand. She would then breathe, and go back to counting.

"Emmaline, fetch every book I have, and bring Marie's as well. Hurry back." She commanded her apprentice, and then she counted the minutes it took her to return. She wracked her mind with a new ferocity, desperately seeking to understand what had cured Torga that couldn't cure Thomas. When Emmaline returned, Natalsa grabbed the books and spread them before her. She cross referenced every blotched notation she had made in Marie's original books to her logs.

"What am I missing, Emmaline?" Natalsa slammed her fist in surrender, and tossed her head back. Natalsa felt Emmaline's cool hand on her shoulder, and was soon embraced by her apprentice. Natalsa cursed back her tears, and refused them admittance into the real world. She would not cry, she would not allow it to happen, because she would know then that she had lost.

"He hasn't yet started the wailing." Emmaline spoke softly, as if scared to awaken him, or give power to her words.

"We are blessed in that regard." Natalsa shook her head.

"There was something different about the day you healed Torga. Tell me about what happened the days leading up to his cure."

Natalsa recounted every detail, and felt that she was rambling by the time it was over. She detailed the sun, the smell in the air, the clothes she wore, and still nothing stood out to her. "I have gone over every detail, and I am certain there is nothing within the genetics of humans versus fauna that causes the remedy to work." She bit her lip until she caused it to bleed. "I could not save your love, and now I am damned to not save mine!" She shrieked until Emmaline slapped a hand over her mouth.

"Stop it now! You were the most brilliant witch of the age, and you are not going to act like a petulant child in front of me!" Emmaline handed her a cup. "Drink, and clear your head."

Natalsa felt her stinging lips and face, and accepted the cup of water. She sighed, and tossed her head back as it rushed down her throat, cool and refreshing. Then she choked, and spat up the water she had drank. "By the powers." She sat up straight. "I've been a fool all this time."

"Teacher?" Emmaline asked cautiously, staring at her.

"The well. Waylan would spend days in the woods, so Thomas said. Surely, he came across the well, and one day was thirsty. What if the well water was corrupted? Was he not the first to contract the Malady?" She felt thoughts rush to her brain faster than she could speak them. "And Torga, why, he drank from the well

-136-

water the last day I treated him. But of course, he had already *had* the malady by that point. And your love, Anthony, he never drank from there, and died as a result." She shook her head. "It all makes sense."

"I'm glad it does to you, but it does not to me. I need you to –
"

"The remedies, while infected, plus well water equals restoration. The well water while not infected equals Malady. Don't you see? It is the one thing I overlooked, and the one thing that makes sense." Natalsa stood. "I must get to the well, I need you to grind up the reagents and primers, have them ready by the time I return. And we shall test my theory, though I lack proof, I am certain I have discovered it. Gods bless us, Emmaline, I think I've done it." She grabbed a bucket.

"Then do not tarry, Natalsa. I will have everything ready by your return." She spoke with urgency and excitement.

+ Chapter Four +

NATALSA RAN TO TORGA and stirred him from his sleep. He shook his heady sleepily and yawned lazily at her. "Rise my friend, we have to hurry." She said urgently into his ear, as she climbed up on his massive back. She wrapped her legs around him as best as she was able and buried her face into his fur. "To the forest, Torga. Be quick."

The bear bounded off towards the woods, and she held fast. The villagers she passed called out to her, but she was focused on directing her familiar. They sped through undergrowth, vines and twisted tree limbs, making a terrible racket as they rushed onward. "To the well, Torga, remember the well?"

The bear huffed and gave a great roar, causing all the birds in the trees above to flutter away in a fright. Natalsa saw the well coming up, and Torga slid to a halt upturning the grass as he slowed down. "Thank you, friend." She kissed him and dashed over to the well. She touched the rocks, again feeling their magic pulsating under her touch. "I was such a fool; how could I have missed this. To think the remedy has been here all along." She wondered about the well's origins as she sent the bucket down deep into the earth and felt the rope cease to descend. She started to pull up the rope and felt it tug, and she felt herself grow excited. Too quickly she pulled on the ancient rope, and with a sinking in her stomach she felt no resistance at the other end of the rope, and knew it had unraveled, her bucket fell to the seemingly bottomless void.

She looked all around the well for another rope, but found nothing. She could of course run back to town, but she was unsure how much more time she could afford. No, if she was going to save Thomas, she would have to do it now. She perched herself atop the well, and began to climb down once more. She sank deeper than she had the first time, and Torga called for her from the mouth of the well, and her fading source of light. She quite quickly no longer felt rocks around her, encircling her, but earth. She kept going, until her feet became very wet, and she realized she had reached bottom. It was quite dark at the bottom of the well, but she felt along the wall and realized it was quite a large open area, perhaps an opening chamber of a much larger cave.

"Perhaps this is no well at all." She said, bending over and trying to touch the bottom of the water. Feeling as she went, she soon discovered the water was no more than three feet deep, for she herself was but two feet taller. Her eyes had somewhat adjusted to the darkness, and she could at least see her hand in front of her, and the sliver or light that showed from whence she had come. It was very cold, and she wondered just how far down she had come. She felt all around for her bucket, and felt time slipping away from her.

"Goodness, how far does this go?" She began to shiver, uncertain of how long she had been down the well. Somehow the darkness made her lose track of time. Her fingers were growing numb and she felt chilled to the bone. Her clothes clung to her skin and she was beginning to stumble. "Where is it?" She screamed, and she heard Torga from a distance roaring back at her.

From the corner of her eye, she saw an unnatural light. She turned, and saw the light was very tiny, but growing ever larger and ever closer. It bobbed along at far too quick a pace to be mortal, one moment it would be close to the ground, and the next it would be at the ceiling where stalactites were protruding from the above like pointed fangs. She took out Thomas' dagger, and felt slightly reassured with it in her hand. She held it firm in front of her, and spoke clearly. "I do not know what you are, but I do not seek to do you harm."

The light was upon her, and circled around her like a moth to a flame. It smelled of Lemonshade grass and crackling lightning. Natalsa nearly fell backwards into the water when she heard the voice. "You could no sooner harm me than you could cast a light charm to end your disorientation." Laughter roared like crashing waves.

"How do you know that? Who are you?" She shouted, quite confused.

The light was directly in front of her, and Natalsa covered her eyes with a free hand. "You live in my house; do you not recognize my fragrance? Or has it been so long that you've spread your own?" It chuckled again.

"Your house?" Natalsa raised her eyebrow and lowered the knife. "Ixtarae?"

The light blinked out of existence. "She was a coward and a thief! You had best raise your knife if you suggest I am her again, I won't be so forgiving the next time!" It cackled again. Natalsa was beginning to get irritated.

"Then you are Marie? What are you doing here?"

"I am here because I could not climb back up the well. You aren't the first person to discover this place you know! When I arrived I cast a light charm, and oh there were paintings on the walls, skeletons on the dry areas, destroyed vellum scrolls, oh it was a witch's dream!"

Natalsa's mouth was wide open, and she suddenly realized just what was happening. She dropped to a knee, and bowed her head. "Hail, Mother. May the Earth continue to bless you."

"Rise, Mother. And may the blessings of the Earth keep you."

Natalsa's heart froze. "Hail, *Mother?*"

"Why yes, isn't that how the Coven's do it anymore? Daughters to the pre-initiates, Maidens to the fertile, and Mothers to those who have or will bear children?"

"I am not but a day passed." She said softly.

"I'm sorry, are you arguing with a ghost witch?" The light flared up again, and lit the entire chamber. For the briefest second, Natalsa caught just a glimpse of the wonders that were down here. There were paintings in red, and unbound, unraveled books lined the floors. Skeletons held onto daggers, and staves, and some of them held nothing but cobwebs.

"Forgive me, Mother. I am merely in shock." She shook her head. "I've never argued with a ghost witch before. This is new."

"You know they figured out what causes children? I can tell you if you don't know." The light buzzed around her face. "Bah, the time wastes. You are on a mission, aren't you? Happen to be missing this?" Miraculously, Natalsa's bucket was floating in front of her face.

"I am yes, but this is the strangest encounter I've had since Kaltyges."

"Well I'm glad to know that I'm still strange enough to beat out a demon!" The cackling began anew, and bounced off all the walls of the cave.

"Mother, for what reason did you come here?" Natalsa urged her.

"The same as you, I realized this well was the source of everything that had gone wrong, and held the key for undoing all of it. I died here, but I knew one day someone worthy would come and I could help them escape where I had failed. Granted, you aren't the first to have made it here. Ixtarae herself is here somewhere, rotting. She is a bit upset that I didn't save her."

"Why on earth not?"

"Wrong intentions! She only wanted to rob from the dead. Always just concerned about her power, and her spells, and ooh look a trinket of Divanis." The light fluttered around in a tizzy. "Hopeless! But you, I can sense greatness in you. And you come for love, and are the bearer of love."

"Marie, I must get out, you have stated truly. But, I have been unbridled in my relations as of late." She said, somewhat ashamed.

"You were a hussy!" She light split in two and rejoined as one glowing ball a moment later. "But this can all be forgiven! I can feel it."

"Can I ask to whom it belongs?" She asked, frightened to hear the response.

"You can always ask! But do not feel entitled to receive an answer every time! I won't be telling you, and in the end I believe you will find that it does not matter. He will be loved."

He. Natalsa felt chills run down her. "A boy?" She grinned, and felt her heart grow warm. "My."

"Yes, yes. I am quite happy for you, congratulations! But, one last thing before I spirit you out of here, and I am going to do so quite happily, though you've been most pleasant company."

"What is it?"

"You have a choice coming, and you will need to choose between Thomas and Estil!"

"What on earth do you mean?"

"We both know I'm not going to answer that, I thought you were intelligent, Natalsa." The light flickered to darkness and back to light, as if the laughter was overtaking it.

"I'm beginning to think the Forks suffered no great loss with your passing." She whispered.

"I have perfect hearing, no matter how well you whisper." The light grew brighter all around her. "I need you to impart a message for me, to all of the village."

"What would that be, oh goodness!" Natalsa shrieked, as she was lifted magically out of the well.

"The world must return to the old ways, and not give heed to new teachers who come promising purity, for these are of a different breed of magic, and the Gods are not pleased with them. You have to tell them. And do not forget, you must make the right choice!"

Suddenly there were no more words, just rushing wind and warmth as she shot up the well chamber with bucket in hand. She rose elegantly out of the well and landed right in front of a very confused Torga. He cocked his head and nuzzled her in greeting. "My friend, you will never believe what just happened." She laughed, and placed a hand on her stomach. "To all of us." She carefully walked back to town with Torga, careful not to spill any of the water.

"That's incredible, Natalsa." Emmaline whispered, as Natalsa poured the water into Thomas' mouth.

"If this is all true, then we have the means by which to cure so many people. The Forks will be legend." She clapped her hands together and held them to her chest. "Oh that this couldn't have been done for your Anthony."

"No, you're going to be. Nobody can accuse you of maliciousness once this is brought to light." Emmaline put a hand on her teacher's shoulder.

"There's more as well." Natalsa whispered now, afraid Thomas would hear. "I would want you to step outside with me for a moment." Natalsa ceased pouring water into the phials of remedies Emmaline had manufactured.

The two witches stepped outside, and Natalsa stared up at the cloudy sky. "I am with child."

"What?" Emmaline threw her arms out. "That is wonderful news, oh I am so happy for you!" Emmaline embraced her. "Don't you think this is a bad time though?"

Natalsa wondered how Emmaline would feel if she found out that it might mean a step brother for her. She decided there that like Marie had told her, it made no difference one way or the other. "You will play a large part of his life."

"His? What do you mean?" She looked at her curiously. T

"Marie and I discussed far more than magic down there. She told me that it would be a boy, and that the way the world is heading right now, that there needs to be a return to true magic. She said the magic of the Seekers is anathema as far as our gods believe."

"Then from whence does this magic come?" Emmaline questioned.

Natalsa exposed her wrists, and showed her the scars. "There is the magic of the demons as well. I received these scars when I banished Kaltyges the demon from this realm. The hell gate was open, and he was being sucked in. He didn't like that I was being left behind, so he clung to me trying to drag me in with him. It burned so badly, and these are the signs I possess to remind me."

"To remind you of what?"

"Of what I can do when I am determined enough. I can split holes in the worlds and protect those I love." She laughed softly.

"Thomas will come through this, and you will give him the chance to be the best father." She grinned. "I just know it!" She hopped up and down comically.

Natalsa felt her insides squirm, and considered telling Emmaline the other part of truth. But it had been one time, and surely fate wouldn't pull such a nasty trick. Especially not if neither of them had meant it. "I should tell you –"

Natalsa's door opened, and Thomas stood against it, though he fell within a moment. "Thomas, you should be lying down. How are you moving?"

"I feel better, at the very least." He paled and vomited all over himself. "Oh that is disgusting." He moaned, and wiped a hand through his sweaty hair.

"I presume I should clean that up." Natalsa cringed, and grabbed a cloth from her bin. "Come here." She helped Thomas to sit, and changed his clothes and wiped his face.

"You had me so scared, Thomas." She whispered into his ear.

"I didn't mean to. It came on so suddenly. But how did you do it?"

He nearly fell on top of her, but she caught him before he crashed into her completely. "That's for another time. Right now you need rest, continued rest. You are weak."

"And you are my godsend." He fell asleep with his head in her lap, and she ran her hands through his hair.

"You weren't meant to die. You were meant to snap me out of my complacency." She kissed his head, and leaned back in her chair.

Soon she too felt her eyes grow heavy, and saw Emmaline douse the lanterns in the home. "Goodnight, Natalsa." She whispered.

+ CHAPTER FIVE +

EMMALINE HAD TO GO see the well for herself, its intrigue drew her closer and her skin burned from being this close to the magic, stronger than any she'd felt before. It was a low humming in her ears that grew louder the closer she narrowed in. It was close, and purest ecstasy.

"She was right around here. We saw her fly out my lord, as only a witch is able."

Emmaline heard voices ahead of her, and stopped dead in her tracks as she recognized Leon's gravelly voice.

"No witch is capable of flight without assistance. But that is hardly the most important matter to you right now." He spoke, and he clapped his hands, causing an explosion to pulse around him, rendering his assistant unconscious. "After all, nobody but me needs to know about this place. Me and the bitch." Leon lifted the man's body, and dropped him into the well.

Emmaline gawked, and hid herself behind a tree. She hoped she wasn't making too much noise, but even the thinnest breath sounded like a hurricane in her ears.

Leon looked around, and then back into the well. He laid his hands on the stones of it, and began to chant softly. "Malia moirbes cachttu mentha." Over and over he repeated these words, until the stones glowed a deep purple. A stream of yellow light flew up from the hole and an unnatural cackling was heard all around the copse in the forest.

"You have no right here, malefactor. Be gone." Came the disembodied voice, which seemed to come from the golden light that Emmaline knew to be Marie.

Leon's face was lined, and he brushed away the light with a flick of his hand. In annoyance, Marie flew around his head, screaming at him. "I gave you a chance. Now know Hell." He screamed and reached out in front of him, and tore a rip in the sky. From Emmaline's perspective, she saw red light pouring out of it, and as she shifted to the opposite side, there was nothing at all.

A scream filled her ears, and she saw Marie being sucked into the tear, until her scream stopped, and there was nothing but normal terrain all around again. "By the powers..." Emmaline swore, and realized what she had just seen, and its significance. "Malefactor." She whispered, only this time it appeared as though it was too loudly.

"Who is there?" Leon shouted, and began to peer about madly. "I will erase you from the living, you had better start to run."

Emmaline considered this to be very sound advice, and she merely sought her opportunity to flee. As Leon looked the opposite way, she made her break for it.

"Ah ha!" He screamed, and she turned around to see him chasing her, running impossibly fast. Soon he was upon her. "So you are alive." He had his hands around her throat.

"No matter. I can soon see to that." His eyes were red and filled with glee, while his thumbs pressed into her throat.

Help me. She thought, and with a great effort, she slammed her hands onto Leon's back, her fire & ice elementals burrowing into him. She smelled the burning flesh before his scream ripped her eardrums.

"DEVIL BITCH!" He swung at her, and missed thanks to the new threat attacking him.

She got up, choking and coughing as she did so, and began to run. "You will fail. I knew what you were, and I have never been happier to be right." She ran. "Your time ends, malefactor." She borrowed Marie's word, and he screamed anew.

"I never knew you had the gift, but then..." he paused. "She has taught you, and if you, then others." He laughed himself, as he expunged her elementals. He gave her chase again, and she could never hope to outrun him. His hands reached for her, and she said her final prayers.

He grabbed her cloak, and she twisted around and felt herself fall into dirt and mud and vine. She was staring at the canopy of the leaves above her, and saw him fast approaching.

"I will enjoy seeing your father's face as he learns of your death, Emmaline. You should never have attacked me." He began to laugh.

Emmaline's fear gripped her, and the only time she had been so scared was as a girl on the night of the Purging. The divine moment when Natalsa had rescued her, but there was no Natalsa this time. And she could not hope to meet his power, there was only... and then the thought struck her. The witch's last defense, the dagger Natalsa had given her all those years back.

She flicked her wrist, and felt it fall into her palm from inside her robe. And as Leon reached down for her, Emmaline plunged the dagger into his ribs. A piercing white light filled the copse and his silent scream broke onto his face. His eyes were wide with pain or surprise, she wasn't sure which, and he fell backwards, scrambling for safety.

"I will kill you here." Emmaline said, as she pulled her robe sleeves back and began to pray.

"You may try." He coughed, as he pressed his palm into his side, and then placed a mark of blood on his forehead. "Vereit allo."

A ring of clouds descended and immediately lifted him far away from her. He rained fire upon the land. "You will pay, Emmaline. You and I will have a reckoning. Ask your bitch about the time in the tent with Estil. It is a tale you would *love* to hear."

And as he disappeared from her view, the rain of fire stopped. She had managed to fend most of it off, but she knew the damage was done now. He carried the knowledge that she knew magic, and though her dagger had wounded him, any man who could command clouds to his side would have little trouble healing himself. If there was to be a reckoning, she had just made a life enemy, and suddenly her elementals seemed like parlor tricks compared to the power he could wield. The only reason she survived was due to the blade once blessed by her teacher. If she was to survive, she would need to exceed Natalsa.

And to save her father, she would need power. Power is protection. And protection is knowledge. She cleaned her dagger and inspected the well. There was no visible damage, but she sensed that it had been corrupted. The humming in her ears was nearly gone now, and the stones felt no more magical than buttons.

Natalsa awoke the next day alongside Thomas, his breathing was steady and his temperature was normalized once again. She inhaled deeply, taking in his scent, and smiled happily. And then she was curled up in a ball outside moments later as an extreme case of morning sickness overtook her. It was miserable, and there was so much vomit everywhere, and her hair fell in her face reeking of it. It was a terrible mar on what should have been one of the most glorious mornings of her life since coming here. She had done it, she had found the cure to the Green Man's Malady and word was already spreading through other villages of her deeds.

People were sneaking their way into the Forks of Elkshead for doses themselves to give to their loved ones, and as it was in the times before the Purging, she was being greeted as a respected woman once more. "Hail Mothers" filled her ears until she heard them in her sleep. Interest in the path of the Witches was growing, and the way of the Seekers were dropping in popularity. She cleaned herself, and without waking Thomas, she left for the market to grab a pastry from her favorite baker.

She was nearly there when she felt icy hands grab her by the neck, though nobody was near. She heard a contemptible voice fill her mind. "Behold, Natalsa, how I will destroy everything you have come to love with less effort than it takes to raise my hands against you." Leon filled her head, and she could feel his loathing pulse through her veins.

She turned, and looked out to where the Seekers had once stood. He was alone, leaning on his oaken staff and grimacing. She saw him rub his side as if wounded, and even then, she could draw no satisfaction from his pain. "What are you doing?" She shouted, and he just smiled and pressed his hand to his throat.

Magically amplified, his voice shook the village. "Citizens of the Forks of Elkshead and surrounding villages, I have come to deliver truth about your miracle witch, Natalsa of the Brim. I am here to reveal all that she has swept under the rug in shame, and to demonstrate why her kind must never be trusted!"

Villagers began to emerge from their homes, including many of her apprentices. Simon, her youngest, came out and had his dagger at his side. "What's happening teacher? Do you need my protection?"

She knelt and kissed him on the cheek. "Your kindness is unfailing. But I fear anything we do to stop him will make us look even more –"

"This woman, has made an apprentice of Emmaline, Daughter of Estil of the Seekers. She has taught her in the ways of magic, while at the same time she took Emmaline's father and taught him the ways of passion! For she now bears a child that would be the apprentice's half-brother! Do you see the insidious nature by which this woman works? She ensnared her enemy and has produced an heir she aspires to use to get control of Estil!"

Natalsa blanched and her pulse quickened.

"What is worse, is she only found a cure for the Malady when it suited her, when her precious bear and side whore were jeopardized! How terribly convenient that now she releases the cure! Isn't it? I have to wonder; did Emmaline or Thomas know of your secrets? And how will they react now, secret bearer? Your most trusted friends weren't so informed after all, were they?" Leon's laughter pierced her, and she began to tremble.

"What other hidden knowledge do you keep in those robes of yours? And what will you do in light of these revelations? What happens when you flee The Forks just like you fled our town?"

She felt her forehead grow hot and her scars began to burn, something that she noticed, had never happened before. The last time she had been so angry was when Delia had been killed. And was that not magic then? She thought to herself, and wondered whether she let herself soak up the energy. She came to realize in those moments that it didn't matter.

"I fled *my* town because of your treachery! Of your insurrection which came about faster than a man's send when his last caress was at his own hand! I have only just learned of the situation myself, with regards to *my* son. You have no right to come here as a black messenger of hatred, *malefactor*." She watched for his reaction, for that name seemed to cause him to lose touch. She was not disappointed.

He hurled a fork of lightning towards her, abandoning control and she whipped up her cloak around her. She had expected the burning, the burning she should have suffered long ago, but the bolt passed into her, lighting her blood on fire. "You, Leon, have been the perpetrator of everything since the Purging, and you and I have a score to settle."

"You settle scores in scores of bloodbaths, did you think I would not know that it was you who killed him?"

She felt her chest seize, and her lip trembled as she watched him hurl Estil's corpse towards her. "You have caused his death, he learned that you bewitched him and could not bear the thought of having a child with you, whore of Kaltyges! His final words were that the boy would be lucky to not be horned at birth!"

Natalsa stared at Estil, and felt her sympathy stir, she didn't believe him to be a wicked man, and her heart broke for Emmaline, who had now lost any family she'd ever had. "You murdered him." She said, as the crowd continued to grow behind her. Simon, Mari, Furler and all her other apprentices were at her side, save for one who ran weeping towards her father.

"Daddy!" Emmaline wailed, as she ran as quickly as she could towards him.

Leon smiled at her. "Do not fret, Emmaline, your father's dying work will save him yet." Leon began chanting, and he withdrew a black phial from his robes.

"Emmaline, get back!" Natalsa turned to Furler. "Draw her in, now!" She shook him by the shoulders as he gawked at her. "Don't think just will it to happen! Draw your emotion and make her come near! Something bad is happening, can you not feel it?" Natalsa turned, and she felt the power of uncertainty and fear take her heart. "Everyone, take shelter!" She twirled around, looking at those who were frozen.

"Rise, and submit to my will, fallen warrior." Leon spoke, and a terrible black glow surrounded him, and it poured out of him and flowed into the lifeless body of Estil. The clouds passed over the sun, and darkened the day, whether by magic or coincidence, Natalsa did not know. With a terror bred of intuition, she removed her dagger, and watched as Furler managed to draw Emmaline back just in time.

For Estil arose, slowly and clumsily, his chin touched his chest as though it did not have the strength to lift itself. But then the corpse began to move more fluidly, and its head rose, and its eyes were embers. Its mouth opened, and without reagent or chanting, it bellowed fire towards them all. Emmaline screamed and threw herself in front of the gathered crowd, and crossed her arms over her head.

A cloud materialized in front of her and a gush of rain swallowed up the fire and all that was left was steam. Natalsa began to pull her back, for she saw her shaking. "Do not lay your hands on me!" Emmaline spun around, and sent a shock running through Natalsa, causing her to fly backwards and fall into the crowd.

"Do you see?" Leon laughed. "Do you see what your sin has done to this relationship? I do believe this girl loved you, it's tragic, and her family loving you seems to have damned them all." Leon wiped away a tear of laughter.

"You will die. And I will do it." Natalsa swore. "I will fulfill this vow today."

"You are mistaken, I am death." Leon stated plainly, and as he snapped his fingers Estil retreated into the earth in a cloud of smoke.

"You are a demon. And unfortunately for you, we have experienced demonologists here to deal with your kind." Emmaline shouted.

"I am as human as you are, and the Seekers have always sought the ways to conquer death. Did you not understand what your father did all those nights?"

"Under *your* orders!" She screeched hoarsely.

"I was but his servant, but now that my most cherished friend is dead, I will willingly wage war against any who have contributed to the state of affairs we are now in. This is the only warning you will receive. Stand with me, or I shall see you killed. But of course, by that point you shall be mine anyway. Choose your sides carefully."

Leon rose into the sky, lifted by clouds and rolling thunder.

Natalsa stared up at him, and the emotions fled her mind, along with them the power she felt growing within her. She despaired in knowing that Estil was dead, for with him had always been the hope of her power being restored, but now all was bleak.

"Natalsa." She heard from behind her, and she turned to face Thomas.

"Thomas." She extended her arms to him, but he fanned them away.

"Prepare your apprentices. We are in for a fight."

"I did not even know what happened with Estil that day, it felt like a dream." She heard the desire to be understood in her voice. She kept repeating herself.

"The same dream my father was under, no doubt." Emmaline stated, pulling back her hair into a long braid of blonde. "But it still does not stem the flow of pain that I am now enduring."

"She speaks truly. We should revisit this when we are not in a state of open warfare with the Seekers." Thomas said, crossing his arms and regarding Natalsa with a look she had never seen before; disappointment.

"Warfare." Natalsa spoke, rolling the word around on her tongue. "With a general who cannot fight."

Emmaline turned to her, and grabbed her chin. "You and I are not done. You have taught me, and now I will teach you how to not be a petulant child whining about how brutally unfair your lot is." She felt Emmaline's hand slap her cheek and tasted its sting.

"I expressly forbid you from doing that again." Natalsa chastised her.

"What are you going to do if I don't? Hex me?" Emmaline said, then she put a hand over her mouth. "Oh wait. You can't."

Natalsa frowned at her. "You best run fast the day I get my powers, or just start running now."

+ CHAPTER SIX +

THE HOUSES WITH YOUNG children were abandoned first, the elderly followed. Natalsa no longer cared if they blamed her, she had more important things to worry over sadly. She held a wanted flyer in her hand, as was provided to her by Mari that morning. She stared at her face looking back at her. She was wanted for crimes of sorcery, and conspiracy to murder. She laughed and crumbled up the paper, and walked up to her building, where she looked out over the land. She was waiting for the armies, they would be here soon, they had left no doubt that the slaughter would begin today.

Furler had gone undercover to the towns surrounding, and had overheard that Leon was going to spend one day and raze the Forks to the ground. He had support, from what Furler had uncovered, yet he was also receiving criticism for lusting over war, and some of his donors had stopped their contributions since Estil's death. Some had whispered that it was an inside job by Leon himself, and the idea was spreading.

The day was nearly spent. Natalsa sat on the edge of the roof and let her feet dangle freely in the breeze. Possessing a small force was one thing, holding magical sway over masses however was another matter entirely. The more he tried to manipulate magically, the more strained he would become. Natalsa held her palm out, and willed fire to dance on it. She stared at her scratched palms and scarred wrists until her eyes began to water, and still nothing manifested.

"It still won't work. I have tried." Natalsa said.

She scrunched her eyes until they burned, and she was certain she would do permanent harm to them. She rammed her heels into the building over and over until they stung. She relished feeling the sensation, so happy to be feeling anything after her continued failures. She reflected on the rules of magic, and hated too little. She thought that with enough hatred she might be able to move a rock from its location to another. But it was not in her to care so little, to give such power to such a useless emotion. There was nothing she could do but continue to fail, and to discover new ways to keep going. She looked to the sky. "What do you want from me? What more can I possibly give you?" She spat.

"You're still not learning, teacher." Emmaline heard from behind her, and she turned to see Emmaline in dark robes, in such direct conflict with her light complexion. "And I know it is not my place to condemn your efforts, or your choices. Please, forgive me for how I acted earlier. I was hurting." Emmaline sat down beside her.

"I should have been honest with you, I wanted to. It was a wedge in our relationship. I was ashamed, and didn't know how to react. I had no intentions of taking your father to bed, the more I try to remember about that day the fuzzier it becomes, and the more my head hurts, right here." She put two fingers to Emmaline's temples.

"You were bewitched." She stated plainly, with no doubt in her voice.

"It would be convenient to think so, and it would relieve me of my guilt. But it was done, and now I have damaged so much in my relationship with both you and Thomas." She laid her head on Emmaline's shoulder.

"Have you not spoken to him yet about the incident?" She didn't sound surprised.

"He will not speak to me." She sniffled.

"How do you mean that? Have you gone to his door and asked him to talk to you?"

"We've been too busy for that, he hasn't slept at my home for the last three nights. I know he is occupied shuffling people too weak out of town, and whenever I try to get his attention, something more important comes up."

"And still, you cannot perform the magic."

"It will not work for me, and after I have taught so many of you my ways, for them to be denied me is a slap in the face."

Emmaline blushed.

"Emmaline, the magic might not come back to me even if Leon dies." Natalsa lifted her head and looked out at the fields before her. Lush and green, without a taint of blood yet spilled.

"You're right. It might not ever return to you." She said sharply.

"There's no need to agree with me so quickly. I can make mistakes." She said, affronted.

Emmaline giggled. "Sorry, I'll show more restraint. Can I make an observation?"

Natalsa opened a palm and shrugged. "It won't hurt."

"The other day I felt something so tremendous, and it was unlike anything I'd felt before in my life. I remember the first time I commanded magic, and it was stronger than that by a hundred-fold. I think that it was you, because I looked at your face, at the uncut emotion, and I got just a hint of what you once were. I was terrified of you, though I love you more than myself, I was scared to death of the emptiness in those eyes of yours."

"I wasn't feeling empty, I was feeling everything." Natalsa crossed her arms.

"And of course, I realized that later. But then I remembered the stories of the Purging, and how you were just before you left town. After they had killed your cat. Do you remember that?"

Natalsa did. "It was residual magic."

"No, it was core magic. I am convinced that under the right circumstances, you could reclaim your magic, and Leon's pathetic demon craft would crumble with a bat of your eyelashes. You just aren't ready to give everything to it."

"I wielded magic since before you were off your mother's breast." Natalsa said, suddenly angry, and in complete understanding of why. Emmaline's words were too true.

"I will let that go this time. But please remember, everything that I have lost has made me stronger. I have very little left to lose. I have lost Anthony, and now my father. But do you know what keeps me from taking your dagger and drawing it across my neck? It is you, and it is this village, and the power that resides within it to restore the old ways. Evil will always attack good, it has the element of surprise. But we have the power of perseverance, and an onslaught of darkness can only stand so long against a cause so powerful. Leon will fall to us, and when you understand everything that you have, the magic will work for you again."

"Are you sure you're but twenty?" Natalsa leaned over and kissed her cheek. "Thank you for your kindness, Emmaline. I made a good choice saving you that night."

"Truly, I believe that Leon wanted me dead that night also. Leon was going to have me killed and blame you, wouldn't it be just like him?"

Natalsa nodded. "I did feel an overwhelming demand to give you my dagger. That seems to have been beneficial. And it would be very like him. But what do you think about his plan to get me pregnant by your father? What purpose would it have served."

"A child born of both magics? You tell me. Has such a thing existed before?"

"Not for a very long time in this world."

"You speak of the Desinders?" Emmaline hissed.

"Yes." Natalsa held her head in her hands.

"Well, I'm sure that won't be the case with your son, it must be Thomas' baby." Emmaline tried to reassure her.

"It doesn't matter. That's what Marie said."

"I wish she would have clarified what she meant that day."

"Isn't it obvious, daughter?"

"It isn't?" Emmaline shook her head and shrugged.

"I was hoping you would have said yes, and then I could have asked you what I was missing. Damn."

"Natalsa?"

"Hm?"

"If I threw myself from these heights, and faced my imminent demise, do you genuinely believe that you could not summon the power to prevent it?"

Natalsa stared at her young counterpart, and doubted herself. "Let us hope we do not have to test that theory any time soon." She knew how foolish it sounded, any day now the Seekers would come with power. And here they were, a smattering of apprentices, with perhaps one truly capable witch. Armed with prayers and hope baskets.

"Simon has offered to lead the children in making Stick Men for luck." She gave a whimsical sigh, and stretched her arms. "I'm looking forward to seeing them in person. I've only seen pictures in your books."

"Certainly anything would help." Natalsa answered, taking out her own dagger and staring at its glimmering edge. She saw herself walking on it, and should she dip too far to one side, she would wound herself and the world could fall with her.

"I will not worry, Natalsa." Emmaline said, leaning her head onto Natalsa's shoulder.

"Then you're a foolish child."

"No, I'm a girl who believes in you." She said as she began to sing.

Thomas had just finished inspecting the walls of the town, and only found a handful of vulnerabilities today as opposed to yesterday's count. His sword and musket swung at his sides, and he was quickly working up a sweat as he refortified the mortar that held the town's walls together. He felt amazing, better than he had felt before the Malady, and thought that perhaps it was simply the renewal of life. He had been sweating a lot lately, and most of it not as a result of labor.

He had no doubt that the child was his, and it was all he and Sheila had ever talked about, having a baby. He had thought that the opportunity for that was long passed for him. But then Natalsa had come, and he had known from the moment he laid his eyes on hers, that she was going to be the rest of his life.

He sat for a moment, taking a brief respite in the shade of a willow tree. He leaned his head back against its bark and breathed deeply. Secured firmly around his neck was a chain, which held a silver band, and it was to be Natalsa's. He pulled it out, and stared at it carefully. He recalled the words that Leon had spoken, and he was torn again. They hadn't been together at the time of that meeting, and perhaps that was the main reason he kept hope. She couldn't have really loved him, after all that had been done to her by him. But then, it wasn't him, but Leon.

He bit his fingernails until he felt a sharp stinging on them, and he peeled back a nail to its bed. It hurt, but it was satisfying. He kept listening for Natalsa's voice, for her to find him and explain it all away. But with every passing hour he realized it would need to be him. He didn't care what had been done before they got together; he only wanted to be everything for her from this moment on.

He did not believe for one second that she would say no to him. He just wished for more fortuitous opportunities to propose to her. He got up, and decided that it was time to stop playing silly games. It was time to ask her, to make her his, and to let everyone who still lived here know it. And once this was all over, they would travel the realm, and restore health to anyone who had been affected by the Malady. It could be a quiet life.

He stretched broadly and smiled, feeling quite joyful in the face of certain hostilities. He began to make his way towards Natalsa's home when he heard the first war horn. He turned towards the sound, and quickly climbed a tree for a better vantage point. Up he climbed, until he was at the as close to the top of the tree as it would allow him without bending in half. He counted scores of troops, and in front of then, were shambling corpses of men and beasts. Leading them, in a glorified red robe, was Estil. And though flames physically lapped at him, he suffered no corruption.

Thomas raised his musket, and squeezed the trigger. "To arms!" He shouted, as he came scrambling down the tree. "They are here! They are upon us! Witches to your places, arms men take rank! They are here! They are here!" And with the light of the setting sun in the backdrop of the horizon, the village of the Forks of Elkshead fell under siege.

✛ Chapter Seven ✛

Natalsa remembered hearing a battle could last all of five minutes, yet seem to stretch hours. As she heard the war horns, time seemed to slow down for her. She was not ready, nor could she ever be, but here she was. She had put on her old robes, the ones with the silver embroidery, and the deep hood. She kissed Torga on the head, and secured her dagger to her sleeve. She clutched a Stick Man that Simon had made for her, and decided to lace a cord around it, and she hung it from her neck for luck. She smudged lavender on her forehead and uttered a prayer. For even though they would not work for her, it was a ceremony for battle, and traditions must be upheld.

She faced Emmaline who wore one of Natalsa's extra robes, and it fit her all too well, and Natalsa felt older. It had been so long ago that she had first met Emmaline, and now here she was almost a daughter to her, in more ways than just the craft. She kissed her on the cheek, and swore to see her when it was all over.

"But where will you be?" Emmaline asked, drawing runes on the back of her hands in silvery paint.

"I will be an extra pair of eyes, and a ready set of legs waiting for opportune moments. As I can offer little else in this fray, maybe I will be the extra seconds someone needs to survive. And yourself?"

"In the shadows, as you were all those years ago, teacher." She said with a tone of respect.

"But why? You have power, you needn't creep." She frowned at her.

"There is comfort in darkness, and the element of surprise." She stepped back. "Good luck, my friend."

The two witches parted, and exited into the streets from Natalsa's home. She worked her way between warm bodies, and said her pardons, as she pushed people aside to make room. There were swarms of orders being shouted, and the smell of smoke was pungent. She heard shouts for the gates to be reinforced, and for water buckets to be kept at the ready for when the firestorms came, yet she passed just as many people carrying buckets of hot oils just waiting to be poured atop unfortunate skulls.

Natalsa navigated the entire perimeter of the town and looked for vulnerabilities. There were certain to be things overlooked, but she hoped to stop someone if possible. The shouts of the townsfolk were ever present, and dogs howled warnings, sensing unnaturalness about them. They sensed the undead, and Natalsa reached back to feel Torgas reassuring snout. "It's okay my friend. We're going to get through this. You are stronger than Delia was, I'd like to see anyone lay a finger on you."

The bear licked her hand.

"To the rooftops!" Someone shouted from close by, and Natalsa stared up and saw several women and men armed with bows and arrows. Natalsa prayed for their keen eyesight, and continued to look for opportunities to sabotage. She saw a rolling orange cloud cover the heavens, and saw violent clouds rumble in. Stinging hail rained down upon them, cutting flesh and searing the wound with salty anguish. She covered herself as completely as possible and heard Torga growl in aggravation. "Where are those witches? Where is our man?"

"Sorry, I was aiming!" Simon shouted, as he began to chant loudly.

"Thank you, Simon!" Natalsa smiled, feeling a great pride in the boy. "Give them everything."

Within a few minutes time the boy had the hail reversed to where it was bouncing harmlessly off their skin, and shots were again able to be fired from the rooftops.

Natalsa heard clinking noises from above and saw her first opportunity at assistance. Grappling hooks were being tossed over the walls of the town from the outside, and she jumped onto Torga's shoulders. She ordered the bear up on his hind legs, and she was easily as tall as the walls herself now, and before too many people could climb up, she was able to cut through their cords. She heard them cursing her, so she knew they were alive and not magic users.

She wondered how many normal people Leon had won over with his prejudices, and felt pity for them. She smelled fires burning, and more smoke rolled throughout the village. She ran towards their source and saw houses burning, and she was immediately reminded of her home on that dreadful night. She ran past the houses, there was little she could do to stop them from burning, but she listened for screams of anyone trapped.

Finding nobody, she was temporarily at a loss of how to help, but that is when she heard terrified shouts of people on the rooftops. "The dead walk!" Cried a villager, who was apparently late to the game.

"The dead also die!" Natalsa shouted to him, "Have your witch hurl fire at them!"

"Thanks, Natalsa!" the man shouted.

More shouts of the same, it was impossible that people were ignorant that the dead were being used, she liked to reason that they were scared simply due to their numbers. And the numbers were enormous. The fetid smells of decay and excrement were overwhelming as the dead pressed themselves against the town.

Reaching in with their cold hands to steal warmth from anyone who dared to get close enough to them. "This is getting absurd." Natalsa said, covering her mouth with her sleeve.

She climbed up, abandoning cover, and leapt up onto a rooftop and began commanding quadrants. "They are less favorable to fire, you must burn them. Remember, seek the blessing of the earth and conjure up warmth until it boils your blood." She rubbed Furler on his back. "Use the elementals; they are there for this purpose."

From across another rooftop, Natalsa watched with pride as Penelope hurled a watermelon sized ball of fire at a group of heavily concentrated corpses. Their strangled cries of anguish filled her with disgust; it sounded like gargling yet reeked of vomit. "Keep at it! All of you!"

"Natalsa, will you let them fight your battles all the day! Or will you surrender yourself and spare them a drawn-out death!" Calvin called to her from across the way, standing high atop a demolisher vehicle. "We have nothing but time, and more qualified magi, this is all sport for us! For me, the reward will be desecrating your body before it goes cold!"

Natalsa felt a rush of wind speed past her, charging the air around her ear with electricity, and she saw Calvin leap out of its path. Mari smiled proudly from behind her. "I finally learned my element teacher." She beamed and Natalsa laughed. "Better late than never, dear one."

Natalsa could hear the sounds of battle all around her, and she was certain hours had passed, yet the sun hung low, and she was amazed to realize it had not been all that long. She witnessed death of her people, but had not seen any of their lot pass, of course, with them commanding the dead it was hard to tell when one person simply got a new deal on mortality.

A loud horn blast was heard from far below on the street level, and Natalsa saw Thomas gallop toward the town's center, waving a large White flag with Elkshead's emblem upon it. "To the front, they press the gates now! The battering rams are gaining strength. Do not delay."

Natalsa found herself looking over her shoulder, and feeling a touch that wasn't there. She continued, following the growing number of people who were rushing to the front gates. The assault was evident on the wooden gate, it was splintering and from the repeated bashings she could see through parts of it. She reeled at the sight of half rotten faces, and gleeful seekers standing behind them giving orders. It wouldn't be long, she knew.

"Emmaline, Furler, Guy, strengthen their resolve!" Thomas shouted, pointing his sword at the gates. "Do anything, we mustn't let them in our walls!"

"We are trying, but even our strength wanes sometimes lawman!" Guy shouted in annoyance, as he was hit with a flaming arrow from the skies. "Mother of God!" he cried, and stared horrifically at his wound, his forearm now holding an arrow firmly in its depths. "Someone help!"

"Witch wounded," Thomas shouted "get him medical attention!"

"The walls will not hold, Lawman!" Natalsa heard Calvin shout, glee in his voice. "Do you know how quickly I will render this town to quavering puddles?"

"The hell you will." Thomas stated, and ran up the ladder to a nearby roof, his musket drawn.

"Furler, help me with the oils." Natalsa ordered him, grabbing him by the scruff of his collar and shoving a bucket of oil into his hands. "They can't ram if their hands are burned open."

"Good thinking, teacher." He smiled, and joyfully sang as he poured the oil upon them. Their screams added an odd overture of dismay to his otherwise pleasant melody.

"You seem to be enjoying yourself."

"To learn something in theory is quite different from doing it in practice. All my life, I have learned in controlled environments. I am, truly, thrilled to be doing something actively for once. Forgive me if I am enjoying myself."

"The gates!" She heard from below, and watched with her mouth agape as the final ram had come crashing through the thick wooden defense. Scrambling corpses leapt up on the gates and descended upon the inhabitants of the Forks. Fire flew from the palms of Natalsa's initiates, and though it thinned their numbers, all it was ultimately doing was weakening them before the magic users entered the fray. For she saw the Seekers were standing quite comfortably alongside Calvin. His grin was unmistakable, and in front of him was the restrained form of Estil. He stared vacantly, pathetically, at her, and she longed to see comprehension in those eyes that once held her attention. She felt regret, and thought of Emmaline, who had been strangely missing for as long as Natalsa could remember.

"This should have ended years ago, witch!" She heard from the distance, and saw Leon sitting back comfortably in a chair under the shade of trees. He was surrounded by Calvin's men, and he drank from a goblet of shimmering silver.

"The journey ends soon, old man." She swore, and was pushed back as calls for retreat were being ordered.

"Get to the high ground! To the rooftops again!" Furler shouted, and Natalsa reiterated his command to anyone within hearing distance. The tide had shifted against them, and Natalsa began to feel sick to her stomach, for it suddenly seemed that his battle had lasted too long, and it was beginning to end. She did not like the way the people fell around her, and how some of them called to her for help as they were torn apart by the corpses. She watched in abject terror as Chubbs rose from the ground, his skull split open horrifically, and his hands extended towards her throat.

+ CHAPTER EIGHT +

IT WAS UNFAIR, he wasn't supposed to die. He was her first friend here, and he was a baker. He was not a warrior, but here he fought. His son was now an orphan. "Oh Chubbs." Natalsa shook her head from side to side, rattling her brains about. She withdrew her dagger and stabbed his temple, eyes staying open only long enough to know where she was aiming. She felt it happen, and covered her mouth.

His legs ceased to support him, and he fell at her feet. She pulled off her Stick Man and put it on his body. "Goodbye to you, friend. I will care for your boy."

Her moment of premature farewell was interrupted by a flood of people rushing to safety, and the dead coming quickly after them. The threat was upon them, and all around her people beat away the dead with pitch forks, clubs, and their fists. It was relentless, for the dead could die, but the living could be brought back by Leon once they had been slain. It was impossible for a husband to kill his wife, and in such ways, did many of her villagers fall, enslaved to uncertainty and cherished love.

She took her share of agony from fighting neighbors that she loved, and one very nearly clawed her eyes out. It was then that Torga had found her and he came barreling through the crowd, knocking enemies out of his way as he battled towards his master. Natalsa had never been happier to see the bear, and leapt onto his back as soon as he was near enough. From his shoulders, she shouted orders to her apprentices to take to the high ground.

From the rooftops the villagers of the Forks were able to wheedle down the oppressive legions of the dead, until the cobblestone roads were not visible due to the innumerable dead and dead again. There was silence in the Forks of Elkshead for the space of half an hour, and everyone was listening for any sign of impending attack.

Natalsa looked out and saw Leon and his men still there, in their spot, but they were eating. Natalsa took the time to see to the wounded in closest proximity to her, and on other rooftops, others began the same ministrations. The respite was too brief, for after what seemed like mere minutes' rapid claps of thunder were heard from above, and what was formerly a bright blue sky was now full of purple clouds. This was the moment that she had been most afraid of, and when her stomach sunk to her knees she barely had the will to pick it back up.

"They come now." Natalsa yelled to the remnant of the village. "Take arms, and –"

"And rip their damned throats out if you've got to!" Thomas called from below, and he pointed his sword to the sky.

The village cheered, more enthusiastically than Natalsa would have guessed, and she found herself cheering loudly along with them. No matter what the next few moments brought, she smiled, and appreciated the village who had accepted her, even at the risk of their own extinction.

"There has been no higher honor." She said to Furler, who had been standing beside her.

"Thank you for showing me how to live beyond the books, teacher." He kissed her forehead and leapt from the rooftop, landing softly on an awning close to the ground. "Rulers of the wind, hear your servant!" He was soon using both of his hands to support a whirling, and growing windstorm. He gave a great shout and sent it spiraling at his enemies.

"Well I'll be damned." She said astounded. "Boy did learn something from me." Natalsa stayed high for a few moments longer, waiting to find an enemy of worth. Obviously, Leon or Calvin would be ideal. But the generals rarely were in the front lines. She saw a man, she thought his name had been Balthus, and she knew that he was on Calvin's side more than any other aide. She had to start somewhere, and there was no better target than him.

"Powers of the Earth, protect your servant." Natalsa prayed, and leapt from the building and landed on the shoulders of people fighting. She fell clumsily, but the people on whom she landed took most of the injury. She quickly scrambled to her feet and locked eyes on Balthus.

"Calvin." Balthus shouted, looking around and back at Natalsa very quickly.

"Mind your tongue before you lose it." Natalsa said, and approached him with her dagger in her hands.

"Altris mensuh calis calie." He shouted, and Natalsa felt her breath being sucked out of her, it was euphoric in a way to start to lose consciousness, and had someone not bowled Balthus over, Natalsa was certain he would have lived. She gave him no time to recover, and she leapt on him, straddling his chest and taking her dagger and plunging it into his ribs, yanking it free with much effort. She then took the blade, and rammed it into his temple, careful to make sure he would not be reanimated.

All around her, she heard people shouting orders, she heard demon tongues, and she saw those she loved falling, despite the protection spells her apprentices wove around them. She had heard a battle was not over until the last breath escaped, but all around her she was finding no way they would possibly overcome these odds. "At least I will die among friends."

She looked around, trying to get her bearings, and as she did she saw the old man enter the fray. Leon was floating above the dead bodies on his signature clouds, and with a wave of his staff he sent an invisible force hurtling towards the assailants. Time seemed to speed up as she saw Furler fly straight into the sky and out of sight, like her familiar on the night of the Purging.

She started to cry immediately, and begged the powers of the air for their blessing. She was screaming as his body began to hurdle towards the earth. Fervently her lips danced with words of supplication, and towards the end of his descent they were demented screams. His body crumbled perversely, and the fear was the last emotion on his face. She could not handle what was happening, and she began to fall back into the crowds.

This was all her fault, she should have surrendered and they would have lived. "Why are you doing this?" She shouted at the heavens. She spat on the earth, and cursed the winds. "Do you want this power to rule? Should I spill my blood here and give myself to him? Fucking work damn you!" She spun around, kicking the dirt and knocking crates and debris over. "Answer me! Years I have gone without answers and before I die I want to understand!"

She took her dagger and slashed it across the scars left on her wrist by Kaltegys. "I banished him at your instruction, I upheld the teachings of our people, and I worked tirelessly to build your glory! You owe me answers!"

The dagger burned hot in her hands, so much so that she had to release it. It fell to the ground and turned to ash upon so doing. She kicked at the ashes angrily and screamed.

She ended up falling, and the grainy dirt being rubbed into her fresh wounds drew her out of her raging. She looked up to finally lay eyes on Emmaline. Her auburn haired, wild eyed apprentice was standing defiantly in front of her approaching father, or at least, what remained of her father. Leon was grinning down at her, ridiculing her.

"He will not kill me. I am stronger than your magic over him!" She spat in Leon's direction, and her arms spanned from east to west for her father. Come back to me Papa. I love you, it is your Emma, please listen to me."

"The fool." Natalsa's eyes grew wide, and she forgot all the frustration she was feeling and jumped to her feet. She was getting closer, but unfortunately, so was the vacant eyed corpse of Estil.

"Natalsa!" cried a villager, and they grabbed her by the shoulder. "Thomas! Look!"

Natalsa scanned the crowd, and eventually recognized the bloodied face of her beloved engaged in a brawler's circle with Calvin. Calvin had a a ring of elementals circling in his palms, and Thomas had his musket aimed at him. Natalsa's heart plummeted, and she quickly turned to see if Emmaline was still alive. Estil was nearly upon her, and Thomas had but one shot. Suddenly, the words of the old witch returned to her, and their meaning resounded with perfect clarity in that moment.

"You have a choice coming, and you will need to choose between Thomas and Estil!"

"Marie, you..." she lacked the words strong enough. "It had never been about love. This is the choice."

Natalsa stamped her foot. "Emmaline, cast a blasted spell! That is not your father!"

But if Emmaline heard, she gave no indication. Natalsa took one last look at Thomas as she admired a daughter who would not give up on her father's love. "I'm coming." She said, and she sprinted for all she was worth towards her apprentice.

She slipped over blood, over bones, and over debris. Broken crates, destroyed weapons, and barrels of upturned ale all served to slow her down. But she could not be slowed. She had made her choice and the crowds parted for her as if she were Torga. She pushed Seekers out of the way, and sent them flying into walls.

"Emmaline!" Natalsa shouted at the top of her lungs, and she dove towards her apprentice, leaping over the bodies of the fallen.

From her peripheral vision, she saw Leon move, and smile. She felt a sting in her neck, and slapped her hand to the spot, feeling a small wooden dart lodged in her skin. The world seemed to slow down as she crash landed into Estil, who went soaring off into a town wall. She heard an unmistakable cracking of bone and rolled to a stop. She ripped out the dart, and found Leon staring down at her. "Your remedy is most useful Natalsa. To the infected, salvation. But to the pure, damnation." Leon bent down and plucked the dart from her fingers. "This batch has been altered to start the Malady much more quickly. Cheers." He said, as he punched Emmaline full in the face with a glowing fist.

Natalsa heard things as if she was underwater, and her vision began to blur, and all her thoughts slowed to sludge. It was all very heavy, she felt the weight of the air on her lungs and could barely press out to draw in more oxygen. It was damning, and feeling all her will collapse, she let her eyelids fall until she was wrapped in silence.

She stirred, though her body burned and she felt weight upon her lungs once again, heavier than ever. She tried to breathe, and felt it burning with even the slightest movement.

She didn't know if she had been unconscious for long, but she looked down at her skin, and saw a green tint already spreading down her arms. She stared up at the sky, still rolling with purple clouds. "I was out of line, of course." She whispered weakly. "In challenging you, spirits. Forgive me." She closed her eyes and a cough wracked her body.

She heard Leon talking distantly, and she overheard him flouting his victory. "Today, the witch has fallen, and she will soon rise as one of my servants. Imagine, the greatest witch who has ever lived, under my control."

"Today, we enter a new world, where we will have order enforced by the righteous, and this woman's power will at last be used for good.

"But first, we must deal with those who would see our return to order upturned. Bring forth the insurrectionists, the girl first." He held out his staff menacingly.

Natalsa was still groggy, but her senses were coming back to her quite quickly. She didn't feel dead, though she had definitely had easier awakenings. She felt her blood pumping strong in her body, and felt the pulse of her heart beating through her veins as she lay on her arm.

The Malady hadn't killed her, though he had meant it to. She whispered, easier now, that it didn't burn as much to speak. This time, she knew what must be done. "Guardians of the skies, bless your servant. Grant me the power to fulfill your wishes, and to protect the old ways. I beg thee."

And for the first time in years, she felt her heart turn to kindling, and her fingertips burn like a furnace. She slowly stood, and played everything quite cool. She turned her attention to Leon, and stared deadpan at him. "See? Look at how dangerous she is now. At last, a witch has a place in the common world.

Emmaline was brought forward, bound by cords and a familiar powder of sage and crushed ivory spread across her forehead. Any power she had was bound to her until she was rid of the cords and smudges. It was old magic, and impossible to break by one's own means. Emmaline stared at her, and her eyes watered. "Natalsa, I loved you. I'm sorry I failed you, teacher."

"Ignorant fool. You betrayed your father and conspired with this seducer. You have committed the most heinous of crimes, and you are to be sentenced to death by flames, administered of course, by my new servant." Leon turned to Natalsa and glared at her.

"Purge her body of impurity." He snickered, and crossed his arms.

Natalsa winked at Emmaline, and the slightest look of curiosity flicked across her face. But it was enough to give Leon warning. But that glorious second, oh.

Natalsa decided against fire, it had recently seemed too favored by seekers. She had invoked the powers of the Sky, and she dispelled the clouds on which Leon hovered slightly above the ground. His fall was not enough to injure anything more than his pride, but when he got up he was already speaking in the dark tongue.

"You obey me, servant, and I command you to kill this girl by the flames!" Leon shouted at her, smacking her with his staff.

Natalsa's hand flew out and grabbed hold of it, and the heat of her palms turned the pathetic stick to ashes in the wind within a breath. "I do not serve you, malefactor." Natalsa whispered, yet it was a whisper that carried over the whispers of others. She was certain her breathing sounded like a summer storm.

"But you are dead! The hex!"

"The hex failed, you perverted your magic, you weak minded charlatan. You really thought it wise to have father kill a daughter who was willing to die? So strong was her belief in her father's love. I was told, recently, that I was going to need to choose between the man I adore more than life itself, or Estil."

She beamed at Emmaline. "At the time I never could have imagined the meaning of that, but tonight it was clear. I choose to selfishly save my lover, or I choose to stop Estil and risk never finding happiness again. I made the same choice I made back home all those years ago, risk myself and save Emmaline. Saving Emmaline has brought us to this point, and I cannot in good faith think that it would send us to ill if I chose to save her again. She is blessed. By giving up everything I would ever have with Thomas, the magic worked for me again, and your curse was broken. It's like she tried to tell me."

Natalsa said, looking at Emmaline and sundering the cords that bound her, and causing a rain to douse her clean of the smudges. "Only when you give yourself to the magic completely will it work for you. And I have never had more to give than I did tonight. By my reasoning, therefore, I have never gained more in return. What you demand in arrogance, I beg for in meekness. Tell me now, whose magic will be subservient now?"

Leon rubbed his hands together, and with a puff of smoke, he was gone from her sight, but the battle recommenced. The hostages broke free of the Seeker's hold on them, and began to fight with a renewed vigor, knowing that their leader was she of legend. "Forks of Elkshead." She sounded, loud & clear over the rabble. "Bind them by righteousness, and use their own methods against them. By sage, and ivory, and cords blessed by my powers."

+ CHAPTER NINE +

NATALSA WEAVED IN AND out of the fighting, seeking only those wearing Seeker robes, other militants had begun to flee. Their magic was no match for hers, but even the timidest spell felt like heaven, and she found herself soaring higher off of blazing light spells. She blinded so many enemies, they fell to their knees, but some threw objects at her. It was no matter now, this time. Let them ridicule her, for at last she had her birthright.

"Welcome back, my dearest friend." She said, smiling as she blazed through the armies.

She heard a loud cracking explosion from close by, and at almost that selfsame second she recognized him screaming, and someone yelling triumphantly. Natalsa turned to see Thomas clutching the barrel of what was his musket, but he was holding it with a bloody stump of remaining fingers, and blood was spattered all over him. Calvin, the bullets intended, was coming closer, spinning his hands in the words of a spell. Thomas could do little more than stare at his blasted stump and gawk in shock.

"Thomas!" Natalsa screamed, vying for his attention for just one moment. He was too far away for her to work magic, not daring to risk hitting him with anything hostile. Calvin was nearly done, Natalsa could tell by the radiating pulse rushing out of Calvin's opened palms. As Calvin opened his mouth to speak a final time, Penelope strode forward and swung a great club at him. The club was clearly under an enchantment, and it glowed with a vibrant sunflower yellow hue, and it connected firmly with his face. Natalsa heard it hit firm, and sent him flying far into the sky in a trailing slipstream of blood. "Powers of the Air, thanks a bunch!" Penelope proclaimed while shaking her club, challenging any to approach her next.

"He didn't keep an eye out for me! He would have been well advised to do so, eh Natalsa?" She shouted.

"That's terrible. Enough of you, I've got a fiend to find. See to it that Thomas is cared for until I return."

Convinced in Thomas's safety, after all - he was in good hands, Natalsa set out to find Leon. She was soon aware of being followed, for the streets were thinning of Seekers, their victory suddenly far less possible.

"You shouldn't be here, Emmaline." Natalsa said. "You might not be prepared for what we have to do."

"Oh Natalsa, I'm so glad you're back in your element. But this started with you and I, and it's going to end with you and I. Here, I don't need this any longer." Emmaline withdrew the dagger Natalsa had given her years ago for protection.

"But, this is yours."

"I've simply been holding on to it until the right day came. Besides, you've given me a far greater power than any I'd ever known until now. I want to avenge my father, and then I can move on, but if you deny me this, I will forever be stuck in this moment, and that will be the end of me. I will cease to improve, and it will be all your fault. We can't allow that, can we?"

"Oh but this has been touching." They both looked up at the same time, and saw Leon standing in front of them, his arms spread wide as if grabbing something. Natalsa felt an old fear crawl up her throat, and a certain burning in her wrists became pronounced. "You have fended off my most dedicated servants, but I will not be outdone by you Natalsa, and neither will my teacher. He has some things he would like to say regarding his imprisonment."

And slowly the ground began to shake, as Leon's hands turned white with exertion, rips appeared in the skies at the furthest ends of his hands. And a purple and yellow light escaped, along with a strong smell of rotting eggs. A cacophony of tortured screams rent the air and Natalsa wished that she could have sent Emmaline far from here, along with anyone left in the town.

Horned, with blackened matted fur, and a pair of gleaming, discerning eyes emerged Kaltegys, the hex demon she bound and banished so long ago. His enormous arms bulged with muscles, with veins running like deep valleys. His row of blackened, fractured teeth flashed at her. "We were far from finished; it is time to answer for your crimes, Natalsa." Kalegys spoke, and his tone was like wind rolling over chasms. It was hard to listen to, for it set her skin aflame, and already the desire to cause death was sinking into her.

"Our score was settled, but I'll be happy to remind you of our arrangements." She threatened.

"I've only been waiting a decade."

"And you don't look a day over old and worthless." She spat, holding up her scarred wrists in defiance. "Let's finish it."

As the demon soared into the purple sky, Leon's followers scattered, screaming for their lives. Waves of demons poured out of the rips in reality, and Natalsa pulled herself up, she felt her blood rush through her body.

"So Demons." Natalsa shouted over the roar of demon song, the unnaturally deep resonating chattering that accompanied these infernals. "They are resistant to all magics except holy, you will need to channel love and direct it towards them. Just like the blessing spells, you must do this Emmaline."

Her apprentice nodded to her, and shouted back. "I'm scared."

"Then let your fear serve you, I believe in you girl." Natalsa said. "And if you get the chance, end him. We cannot let him live."

"Kaltegys or Leon?"

"Yes." Natalsa nodded.

"Hail Mother."

"Hail Daughter." She responded, embracing Emmaline.

The two witches ran off in opposite directions, Natalsa was uncertain if she'd live to see her again.

Emmaline was following the feeling of Leon's magic, and it was easier now that there were fewer Seeker's around. Though all around her, she saw that many of the Seeker's saw Leon's end imminent, and they had taken to looting, burning, and when they thought they could get away with it, raping.

Emmaline was rushing through the streets, smelling the air, feeling the ground, and could tell he was close. Her head turned quickly at the rattling of empty jars rolling down an alley, and a bird cawing nearly ended up with her frying the beast. She fought to compose herself and control her breathing; hasty magic would end up hurting her.

She heard a cry for help, looked around to see a woman being dragged into the back end of a shop, her legs kicking as the door closed. She caught a glimpse of someone resembling Leon rounding a corner, and heard the woman scream again. "Dammit." Emmaline said, and turned towards the cries for help.

Emmaline busted down the door and was surrounded in darkness. "Rulers of the Sky," she began, but the wind was knocked out of her. She felt herself being beaten by clubs; over and over they rained down on her. She covered her head with her arms and scrunched her body as tightly as she could. She screamed and fought to recall the utterance to a spell, but they were unceasing. It had been a trap. She repeated it to herself over and over, until she started to slip into darkness.

"Stop..." She begged, her words falling on deaf ears. "You're killing me..."

She heard their laughter, and she thought of her father, of Anthony. Their strength filled her, and as the last crash of the club came down she rose and a pulse of energy sent them crashing into the corners of the room. She felt tremors rolling down her body, and felt dangerous.

"Light." She snapped, and the room was illuminated bright as day. She saw two seekers, old men nearly with gray hair, crumbled in the corners. "Your kind do not have the spirit of magic, you abuse it." She knelt and grabbed one of the men and gripped his jaw so he looked at her. "And may the magic abuse you from this moment forward, unless you surrender your hold of it. By the authority of the elements, I bind thee." Emmaline said, and licked her finger, placing a quick sigil on the forehead of the man she held.

She heard the other man get up and was gone before she could get to him. Fortunately, her ice elemental was faster, and the man fell and slipped, landing on his forehead with a profound crack. "Consider yourself fortunate, some people don't get second chances." She said, getting up and slapping him across the face.

She was able to leave, though her muscles screamed at her to stop with every movement she made. Her muscles pulsed and her face was bleeding now. She felt as though she would have knots on her head for weeks to come, but the knowledge that Leon was losing everything gave her the will to move on. She just needed to go a little further, and she would have him.

Most of the demons she encountered had been off terrorizing people, and they were terrifying. She saw people getting spiked and roasted over flames of the brightest purple. The sickening smell filled her nose and she fought back nausea. She was getting anxious, and when she didn't feel Natalsa's dagger, she knew a moment of regret for returning it to her. But then she heard him, and his voice accelerated her courage.

"I do not care, Balthus. I need to get our remaining men out of her and we need to regroup if we are to survive."

"I've told you my lord, the men are finished, they have cried off your teachings, nobody expected or wanted *demons* again."

"I have no room for cowards in my ranks." Leon said, and Emmaline saw him jab his fist through Balthus' chest. She clapped her hands to her mouth and tasted fear in the blood that rolled across her tongue. "I can't finish him, he will kill me."

Leon turned, startled at first, and then his face relaxed as he saw who it was. He began to churn the air around him, and he sent a series of crackling bolts straight towards her. "You have been marked for death for years, why do you continue to live!" He sent another curse at her.

She rolled out of the way and tasted dirt rush into her mouth as the bolts flew harmlessly past her. "Guardians, hear your servant. Let me know what to do." She stood up, and approached him, without elemental, or plan. She was just a girl with a belief.

"You have twisted magic to a realm where it ought never have gone. And look at the evil that you have caused. This is all you, Leon." She shook her head sadly.

"You were someone's beloved once, how could you do this to the world? To other living creatures who have families, and feelings, hopes and dreams? Before you try and kill me, just please let me know why. Tell me that you are not such a monster."

"You want to know why?" He laughed and shook his head bemusedly. "Fine, witch. Before I kill you, not try, before I *do*,I will tell you.

"My mother." He said, after a long pause. "My mother was dying, and the witches would do nothing, claiming that it was the will of the powers. She was but thirty years, and all I had left in the world. So when she died, and I knew the witches would not intercede unless it benefited them, I delved into the other realms of magic, to learn what I could to stop the death from happening again to someone I loved. And now, because of your father, I have succeeded. What more do you need to know?" He began to make lighting crackle from his fingertips and rush down to the earth at his feet.

"Someone loved you. And you could be loved again, look at this. You've done all this to stop the powers of death, yet because of you this village and world has seen more losses I'd wager than it would have naturally. You are the harbinger of endings, and I think your mother would be ashamed of what her boy has become. It's not too late to give this up, Leon, you will never be innocent of these atrocities, but there can be redemption even after the longest fall."

He looked at her, and she watched his hands for the slightest hint of movement, and he took a step towards her. He began to speak when a surge of electricity pulsated through the clouds above, and a din of screaming unlike anything she had ever heard filled the air. Gusts of wind sent her and Leon flying backwards, and as she flew backwards, she saw Leon smack into a wall and slide down it unconscious, a second later, she knew blackness.

+ Chapter Ten +

NATALSA HURLED BOLTS OF energy at Kaltegys from her position, and he rashly smacked them back at her. Fortunately, the holy light only strengthened her resolve. "You forget everything, don't you demon? I'm your opposite, get down here and fight as if you earned those wings instead of acting like you ripped them from a greater infernal!" She hoped he would come down, she had scars to repay.

Kaltegys swooped down at her, and she smelled sulfur and ash as he roared past, lifting her up by her shoulders. "Let's see if you land on your feet like your cat did."

Natalsa dug her fingernails into his oily, feverishly hot skin. "You were wrecked by my kitten; your pride must be so hurt. You should meet my new familiar, if you thought my kitten was bad."

Kaltegys released her, and as she felt herself slip, she grabbed fast onto his legs. Down they went, and Natalsa twirled with him from the greatest heights. "If I fall you're coming down with me." She hissed at him, and he flapped his wings, slowing their descent just enough.

"I bind you, Desinder." Natalsa said, as her feet found sanctuary on solid earth. "And I will see all the nether realms closed. Retreat now, while I still am building my strength." She ordered the demon.

"Come with me, let me show you a world that witch & demon could make. I promise not to treat your corpse too badly!" He screamed, and his unceasing chattering filled her ears again and made them buzz.

"Forces of righteousness, I invoke th—" She felt Kaltegys' fist connect with her head and she went toppling backwards into a pile of corpses.

"I will never go back. This time, I will banish you, and you will know unending torment at the hands of the makers."

He raised his cloven feet high and smiled maniacally down at her. "Farewell, Natalsa of the Brim."

Natalsa rolled out of the way just as his hoof came smashing down near her head. She breathed in and prayed to the holy powers, and laid hands around his ankles. Slowly he began to feel the burn, and though he kicked she refused to let go. "I made a mistake not ending you before, I will not be shackled by your legacy again. It is time you earned scars of your own!" She listened to his screaming become more and more pained, she was certain it would be a sound she could never forget.

"Elis matus vina vinay!" Kaltegys shrieked, and a host of demons came to his aid, with black skin as though they had come from piles of charcoal.

"By the power of light I release you from damnation, seek your eternity!" Natalsa shouted, and his allies disappeared from the sky.

"Mercy, fine, I cry mercy! Please let me live, tortured though it may be!" Kaltegys cried to her. "I will take my magic and return from whence I came!"

"I would sooner die than trust you, for it would come to the same." Natalsa hissed, grabbing him by the shoulders and staring into his perilous eyes. "You forget, I know exactly how you operate! You fill their heads with these thoughts, these *sins*, and this is what the world becomes. You are not worthy of mercy, you are not fit for a single tear drop of mine." She was in full awareness of what she was doing, and focused all her energy on her hands. They began to glow, and Kaltegys started to wail in terror.

"Natalsa, I beg thee, I am sincere!"

"You are sin, now sear." She drove her hand into his side and grabbed hold of his insides. She felt the vital organs begin to sizzle and felt the steam rolling up her wrist. "I am done with demons. So finished with your ilk." She dragged him back to the rips in reality, and turned his head to gaze at the tears in reality.

"Take a message back to your fellows, tell them this is my world, and that you nearly won. But you were undone by me yet again, maybe this time they'll kill you and put you out of your misery."

She summoned all her strength, and threw him into the gaping hole, screaming the whole way as she did so. Years of regret flew away with him, and at the expulsion of their master, the lesser demons soon flapped their leathery wings and followed him back into the abyss, shrieking and chattering all the way.

The tears in reality were unclosed, but nothing came from them except the billowing smoke trails and sulfuric fumes. Natalsa placed her hands at the furthest reaches of the tears, and knew the burning yet again. She strained, and little by little the holes began to close, but it was strenuous, and her muscles burned. She heard the howling from within, and they were very nearly closed, when Natalsa felt herself get pulled forward, as a hand grabbed her chest. "This time you will suffer with me!" Kaltegys shrieked, and Natalsa felt herself being pulled in.

The rich tones of earth were giving way the further in she went. The smell made her nauseous and her head was spinning, nothing seemed balanced. The chattering of Desinders grew louder, as they cheered Kaltegys on. She toppled over into the portal and felt herself falling so far down. Kaltegys was holding onto her firmly, joyously shouting his supremacy above the other demons. "She is ours! The woman is ours!"

Natalsa landed roughly on a scorched orange ground. She was surrounded by demons, and imps, and all manner of dark beasts with fearsome black eyes, shining like hematite. Their teeth were bared, and their hands were ready for play. "I told you she was a pretty one, for a human, now we can have our way with her one by one. She will breed the new demon race, and we will have our chances again. For they are always greedy, and self-serving, the humans. We will be patient. We will reap." Kaltegys foamed at the mouth, his side gushing yellow putrid ooze.

Kaltegys pinned her down, and tore at her robes, trying to remove them. "She will be mine first, she owes me favors after all this time."

Natalsa's lips curled in revulsion and she brought her forehead slamming into his, knocking him back. "I will throw myself off this earth before I let your perversion upon me, you foul fly among hornets."

Kaltegys approached her, eyes full of murder. "You –"

A loud invasive laughter filled the air, and all the chattering of the lesser demons ceased at once, and they dove behind rocks, and dug themselves holes, while others flew confusedly in circles. Natalsa felt the shadow fall upon her and quavered as wave after wave of dread overcame her. Knowing she was dead, more certain than anything else, she dared raise her head to see what was coming. A demon unlike any she had ever seen towered heads over the other demons, and its skin was black and purple, rippling with shimmering scales. Its horns, though grotesque had an elegance that entranced her, and his face, despite being terrifying, filled her with a deep sense of awe.

"So you are she. Natalsa of the Brim." He spoke, his voice echoing all around her and shaking the ground. Kaltegys began to fly off, but he was stopped in midair by one of the new demons bare hands grabbing his wings and holding him fast. "Kaltegysuaranamathez, you will find the healer at the spire. Treat your wound and you and I shall discuss much."

Natalsa stared open mouthed at this new beast, and could not help but fall to the ground. This was surely a power of demons, a god of their people, and she knew death was imminent, but to be so close to one of the originators of the earth begged her to be respectful.

"What are you doing, child, get up and act as a woman of your standing." He commanded.

Natalsa turned her eyes slightly toward him, and pointed at herself questioningly.

"Yes. Stand." He boomed, and he knelt beside her. "I am Raytheon, in your tongue. Raytheon, of the infernal air. Ruler of these realms, and those entrapped here. I would speak to you, as an equal, and in perfect trust."

Natalsa could hardly believe what she was hearing. But she reasoned, if she was to die, this Raytheon surely had the means to do so without toying with her. "Hail, Raytheon." She stood, and bowed clumsily.

"It is my understanding that there is a human above who is the reason many of my children are not returning home tonight. Leon, I've been informed, is his name."

"It is so."

"Is it?" He laughed. "Tell me. How have the atrocities he's committed to mine, compared to yours?"

"I'm not sure I can explain all of that in a quick fashion." Natalsa stammered, still in awe of the size of him.

"We don't need all the details, woman. Just the crux."

"He was solely responsible for the death of hundreds of witches, he has cost a young girl her lover and father. He orchestrated the death of countless others, and has perverted the dead. He is the most heinous villain I have ever seen."

"And so he deserves this place, and you do not." Raytheon pondered aloud. "Do you agree?"

"I do not like to inflict suffering, but sometimes it must be so. If lives hang in the balance."

"He is a foulness, and he has angered me. I want you to bring him to me, and I want him to know such exquisite retribution, Natalsa. Each day here lasts a thousand of your human days. I owe him pain. I am offering you a trade, his soul, for yours."

"I will trade him to you, so that you may exact your vengeance. On the additional condition that henceforth the dead do not rise, regardless of the invocation. The magic Kaltegys inspired must remain in this realm; it causes too much damage in mine."

"And what benefit would I receive from such a thing being performed?"

"I vow that I will not return here with a trained regiment of my apprentices, and see this realm destroyed. The lives of my people hang in the balance as long as this realm exists. And though I do not like to see suffering, I far value my life above any of a Desinder. No offense intended at you, you have been more sensible than I could have hoped. And if all were like you, perhaps we would have better relations."

Raytheon remained silent, and Natalsa saw other frothing infernals looking back at him to her to see what would happen.

"I do not know if you have the powers of that magnitude, but if any human would, I would believe it of you. We have a deal. I will remove the magic that reanimates the dead. I will return you to the surface, and you will bring me him, alive."

"We are agreed." Natalsa said.

Raytheon stood and clapped his hands together, and Natalsa felt herself shoot upwards in a rush of warm air.

She shot through the ether and saw blue skies with hints of purple clouds lingering. Fresh air, clean glorious air rushed into her lungs and a pulsating yellow flash ran across the sky.

"Rules of the earth, I seek he who has caused such agony. Bring me to Leon, that I may end his plague on this realm. Hear your servant. I beg thee."

And from her chest glowed a radiant star, it flew from her and danced down the street, bouncing off walls and stone. She rushed to keep up with it. "Here I come, you sick bastard. Your ending is at hand, and I will know peace at last."

Natalsa followed her star, and entered a blasted opening, with scorched earth and broken crates scattered on the ground. She took a quick look, and saw Emmaline unconscious along with Leon. Natalsa went to Emmaline, and felt for a pulse, and found one strong and resilient. "Apprentice, wake up. I need you to help me end this."

Emmaline's eyes opened, and she stared up at Natalsa. "Oh, oh thank heaven. I remembered a light, and thought you must surely have died. For no other exit would be suitable for you, teacher." She embraced Natalsa.

"I'm not dead yet. Come, we have a bargain to uphold."

"A bargain?"

"Help me carry Leon, and I will explain." Natalsa grabbed his upper body. "There's this demon lord that Leon has upset quite badly, his name is Raytheon."

And so Natalsa explained, and she was shocked to see Emmaline's resistance. "Natalsa, we could bind him, and spare him that damnation."

"He is too dangerous, Emmaline. He could never be trusted."

"Yet you would trust a demon, who could train Leon up to be more fearsome than he is already?"

"Demons do not have any need of powering up humans, our magic cannot compare to theirs in the end."

"Unless it is a child of both magics." Emmaline hissed, heaving Leon's body ever onward.

"Do you want him to be your brother? Damn it woman, nothing these last few months have made sense and yet you treat me as if I orchestrated the entire affair. Trust me, I would much rather be having Thomas in my bed than be grappling with your father. His size is hardly considerable."

"Oh my, stop." Emmaline said, gawking at her. "I don't need those images in my head. I'm just saying can we trust Raytheon to uphold his end of the bargain? And just enjoy Leon, or do you think he'll eventually get bored and seek our blood again?"

"If he does, we will be ready. I think we should train more people, you and me. We are going to need to raise up a lot of followers to resurrect our order. I would like you to teach with me, Emmaline."

The two witches carried Leon to the holes in reality, where the unnatural screaming and chattering was nearly deafening.

"Alright, I agree with you. I'll do it." She looked at Leon. "Though you should have earned my loathing, I pity what's about to happen to you." Emmaline said, and looked at Natalsa.

"We will toss him in. The demons will see him, I am certain of it."

"And what of the portals? Will they close?"

"If they do not, I will teach you a new lesson today."

Into the rifts they lowered Leon's body, and just before he was completely inside, his screams tore at Natalsa's eardrums. "No! No! No!" He screamed over and over, and his shouting became more urgent once he was inside. The tears in reality began to heal and before her eyes the rifts were sealed, and Raytheon could be heard uttering his thanks.

+ Epilogue +

IT TOOK THEM DAYS to cleanse the town after the siege had ended. The remaining villagers were still finding splotches of blood and bits of bone a week after the battle had finally ended. Slowly, curiosity called the old inhabitants of the Forks of Elkshead back home. They were welcomed back, and their flight forgiven as if it had never happened. The village had become a hub of activity after Leon's, and sequentially the Seeker's fall. From across the land, everyone came to see the town that had turned away manifested evil, and had been the reason that the Green Man's Malady had been cured.

What inhibited them before, the Seekers, was done, and the prejudice against witches was all forgotten after witnessing what evil had attempted to take their place. Natalsa and Emmaline saw the construction of a new building, the school of the Elements, the first school of its kind in all the world. Thomas, now down to just one hand oversaw the construction while they were busy. He carried a sword alone now, having had his fill of Muskets. He stood by Natalsa the morning the school opened, and gave her his ring.

The school quickly gained a reputation for producing quality students, and within several months they were gained more students. Emmaline and Natalsa spent much time deciding over what must be done to assist with the teaching of so many. It was decided that Emmaline would be the leader of the second school of the elements in her old home of Whittle's Bend. It was surreal for her to return and see the place where her father had toiled, and so much of her life had ended and begun.

She burned down the town hall on her first day back, and employed reformed Seeker's in the cleanup of the ashes and rubble. She would not spend one night near such a dreadful building where her father had been manipulated so. The townspeople who had fallen under Leon's bewitchment finally saw clearly, and begged Natalsa to forgive them of their crimes.

She had her doubts that some of them were sincere, but for most the town, she offered forgiveness. Though she never returned to Whittle's Bend, she thought of it frequently, especially in her later months of pregnancy. It became harder and harder to move with each passing day, and eventually Natalsa just stuck to staying in bed hugging her blankets.

Furler, Penelope & Guy administered the teaching of apprentices while she was in her last days of her pregnancy. Thomas was often seen pacing about the house, doing yard work, tumbling around with Torga. Until one morning when he made a mad dash on horseback to Whittle's Bend. He pounded on Emmaline's door and drew her out of a restful sleep. She awoke at once to his pounding, and understood its meaning. "I will be right out!"

They raced back to the Forks of Elkshead and made it there just as Natalsa's water broke. "Okay, I'm here; you can officially go into labor now."

"I'm glad I have your approval, Emma." Natalsa whimpered, holding onto her hand tightly.

"Here, hold mine. It's not much but it's the only one I have." Thomas offered, but Natalsa turned him away.

"You've lost one already, I won't have you lose another."

The labor was unlike anything she had ever endured, and as the sweat poured down her face and onto her chest, she took one last deep breath and then heard him cry for the first time. He was red and wrinkly, and after being cleaned off carefully by Emmaline, he was handed to her in a white swaddling cloth.

"He's gorgeous, Natalsa." Emmaline said, and she smiled at the small boy.

"Let me hold him." Thomas asked, after Natalsa had held him for what seemed to be forever. "Come here my boy." Thomas said, and kissed the baby's forehead.

"He was worth every sleepless night."

"And every sleepless night to come, I'd wager." Emmaline smiled. "What have you decided to name him?"

"Marin Ter'ima." Natalsa said.

"Marin I understand, but Ter'ima?" Emmaline said, speaking the name over and over. "I can't remember you ever mentioning that name, what is it?"

"I don't know, but it's held my attention for weeks now. And Thomas has been nice enough to let me choose any middle name I wanted for the first born. He's such a good man, aren't you stumpy?"

Thomas smirked at her. "You can call me whatever you want now, he is wonderful."

In the months that followed the birth of Marin strange things happened in the Forks of Elkshead. The foliage around the town began to flourish, and the waters became clearer than they had ever been. It appeared to Natalsa that he was going to be far more than an average boy, and the only time the boy ever fussed was when he was where the rifts in reality had been torn. She pondered, and fretted over what that meant, but as far as she was concerned, Thomas was his father.

Even when his facial features resembled more and more of Estil, Thomas kept stating how handsome his boy was. Emmaline had the greatest attachment to him, outside of his parents. And she would often spoil him by taking him on rides through the woods on in her arms. Marin giggled most near the well where the remedy had been discovered properly, and Natalsa found many reasons to spend time there. It was again a place of peace, and often Torga would come with her and sniff around where his honey used to be in such abundance.

The boy lacked no guardian, for he was a child of the Village, and he represented hope for every one of them. That he was walking by 7 months was a wonder to nobody, nor that he was speaking by a year. It seemed only natural that his command of magic would begin to show itself, and by his first birthday he was able to light up his dark bedroom simply by smiling.

"He is unquestionably powerful, and though I want to say it is because of me, I worry." Natalsa confided in Emmaline who was combing the boy's auburn hair, so similar to hers.

"The only thing that matters is showing him love, if we love him, it does not matter under what magic he was conceived."

"Does it bother you? I know before, I had your forgiveness, but seeing him as he is?" Natalsa watched him walking and grabbing hold of twigs near the well, and soon after running into Torga with a shout.

"Nothing about that boy could ever bother me. I have family, a direct link to my father. And I have you and Thomas, and that is enough for me."

"Is there no one who has caught your attention? Nobody to hold you in the cold of night, Emmaline?"

"None compare to what I lost. Perhaps I am simply not meant to love again."

"I hope that isn't so." Natalsa said, holding her arms out for Marin.

It was pitch black that night, and Emmaline was sound asleep in her tiny bed above the school. She was awoken from her sleep by a noise downstairs, and she called to mind a spell. She walked quietly downstairs to see what was making the noise, and found an eerie glow coming from under the door. It glowed brighter, and brighter, until it could have been midday. A gentle knocking was heard on the door, and she heard her name being called gently in a way it hadn't been called in many years.

"Emmaline." She heard her name spoken, and she caught her breath as she turned the door handle.

There he stood, as perfect as he had been since before the Malady had claimed him.

"Powers of the Earth...Anthony!" She exclaimed.

+ ACKNOWLEDGMENTS +

I would like to thank my readers who have picked up this book, whether you found it online, in person, or perhaps under a rock! You reading this makes my hours of work worthwhile. So, thanks!

Another special thanks goes to my cover artist, jerry8848 and Wolfke74 of Deviant Art. They were gracious enough to let me use their enchanting piece "Looking for Magical Wonders" as my cover image. Thanks you two!

I also can't forget Dan Bechler. Dan helped me understand weaponry (but especially muskets) in the time period my novel was set. He explained how accurate these things were, and how much damage could be expected from something going terribly wrong.

I would like to thank my beta-readers, without whom, this book would not be nearly as good. So, to Meghan Richardson, Briana McClendon, and Molly Ripberger. Your input was invaluable.

Many people ask me how they can help me as an author. The simple answer is leave an honest review! Reviews help new readers determine if my book is worth their time. I love reviews on www.amazon.com, and also www.goodreads.com.

Want more? The second book in the series is called "Sisterhood of Terima" and is scheduled to be completed by Fall of 2017. This story will follow the world after the fall of the Seekers, and it will show you how the world moved on after nearly being ripped apart by this chaotic order.

For more information, please visit my author page at www.facebook.com/cmcfiction for regular updates.

MORE BOOKS BY CHAD MCCLENDON

YOUNG ADULT

Lipstick Trace – A story of two unlikely friends who form a glam rock band in the early 2000's. Together they overcome questions of love, identity, and how to overcome a dark past.

Available at www.myBook.to/lipsticktrace

HORROR

Uploaded Vengeance - On a dark Halloween night in Salem, a grandfather takes revenge on the bullies who led his grandson to kill himself. Torture, shame, and ridicule await the teens who underestimate this old man, who has a secret of his own.

Available in One Night In Salem, at www.fundeadshop.com